Point

SUNDOWNERS

UNDERWORLD

James Swallow

SCHOLASTIC

Scholastic Children's Books,
Commonwealth House,
1–19 New Oxford Street,
London WC1A 1NU, UK
a division of Scholastic Ltd
London ~ New York ~ Toronto ~ Sydney ~ Auckland
Mexico City ~ New Delhi ~ Hong Kong

First published in the UK by Scholastic Ltd, 2001

ISBN 0 439 99904 9

Typeset by
Cambrian Typesetters, Frimley, Camberley, Surrey
Printed by
Cox & Wyman Ltd, Reading, Berks

10 9 8 7 6 5 4 3 2 1

1: THE BURNT HILLS

The night air was sweet and dry to Sleeping Fox, filled to the brim with scents and wisps of taste. The aged Indian rubbed a hand over his face, his tough, leathery skin like sun-baked parchment, and breathed deeply. He smiled as he dropped to his haunches by the campfire, the small knot of flame casting dashes of orange-yellow light over his tepee. The old man did not look up as the coyote padded gently into the circle of firelight, the milky orbs of his blind eyes long since sightless. The animal dropped the corpse of a desert hare at his feet and cocked its head.

"Ah, thank you, my brother. It is so hard for me to hunt with these old bones." Sleeping Fox made short work of the hare, skinning and preparing it on a makeshift spit over the fire. "Shall I tell you a story while we wait for our dinner, Coyote?" he said conversationally. The dog yawned and settled down on to its paws, watching the old man through half-open eyes.

"There is a wanderer like you who hunts across

1

the land as we sit here," began Sleeping Fox, "a young man named Jonathan Fivehawk." The elderly shaman smiled. "He is pure of heart and strong of will, chosen he is by the Great Spirit to do a great deed. To end the tyranny of The Faceless."

The coyote's teeth bared in a low growl, his ears flicking up.

"No, no," said Sleeping Fox mildly, "not here, old friend. Many miles away." He sighed. "It was difficult for him to accept his destiny at first. He is a son of the Ulanutani tribe, those who walk among the People along the Spirit Path, always wilful in their ways. He searches for his sister, lost to the minions of The Faceless, the great evil that slumbers in the earth. The legend chose him, you see."

The old man paused, using a stick to stoke the fire. "The Great Spirit put him on the path he now walks, but also told of another who would join him, one not of the People. A white man." The fire began to build, and amid its flames danced images, flickers of light and colour that formed into faces, landscapes, animals, objects. The coyote watched with interest as two men appeared in the heart of the fire – one an Indian with serious eyes and a watchful face, the other a white man with an easy smile and a cocky turn to him.

"Tyler. A boy become man, once hunted like a beast by his own people but free now, free to walk his own path, to search for the blood of his blood like

Fivehawk. Tyler seeks his uncle, you see." Sleeping Fox reached out a hand and stroked the coyote's head gently. The fire began to pulse from within; more visions flickered inside the streams of flame, a street empty of life, houses and stores all barren and empty, a ghost town.

"The minions of The Faceless came to this place and took its people, just as they had done a dozen times before, but they reckoned without our two braves." The coyote watched Fivehawk and Tyler ride into the vacant street, saw them fight a man who seemed to wear the wings of a carrion bird, saw them free a hundred humans who moments before had been like mindless, blind cattle. "Fivehawk is troubled," the Indian added with a sigh. "He sees himself defeated in the midst of victory, even as he draws closer to that which his enemy holds dear."

The wild dog glanced up at the old man, a questioning murmur in its throat.

"Yes, my friend. His companion does not yet believe in the darkness that lies in the shadows, although he soon will. He sees only the outer shell, the husk of the beast, like the shed skin of cousin rattlesnake. Tyler will meet the minions of The Faceless and be tested." The flame wavered, the ghostly image of a hairless head with obsidian glass across its eyes appearing, then fading. "This will be. He will find the blood of his blood or fail." Sleeping Fox looked up at the sky, towards a group of stars, his sightless eyes seeing nonetheless. "Both must succeed, you understand? If they fail before the stars are right, the world will drown in darkness." He scratched the coyote behind the ear. "And you and I will starve."

The old Indian banished his serious expression with a smile, reaching for the roasting hare. "Come now, Coyote. Let's eat."

Fivehawk surfaced from sleep with half a word on his lips. The Indian blinked and hesitated; no, it was gone, the thought vanishing like smoke from his mind. He glanced over at Tyler and was mildly surprised to see the young cowboy awake and looking back at him.

Tyler yawned. "I could've sworn I heard someone saying my name."

Fivehawk nodded but said nothing. The same feeling had occurred to him. After a moment, he stood, picking up his blankets from where he had been sleeping and rolling them up. He pointed to the horizon, where a line of faint light was slowly growing. "Dawn is near. We should get on our way."

Tyler gave a strangled groan. "Do you even understand the idea of a lie-in? We've been riding for days, dawn to dusk. Would it kill you to let me get some extra sleep once in a while?"

Fivehawk ignored him. The white man seemed to be comforted by his own complaints.

4

"At least let me get some coffee first. God knows, I can't get started in the morning without—"

"A cup of coffee as black as pitch," interrupted Fivehawk. "Yes, so you say every morning."

For want of a better retort, Tyler made a face at the Indian and got up, alternately rubbing the aches out of his limbs and mumbling darkly about how some folks had no right to be so darn perky in the morning. He snatched up a cup of cold coffee left over from the night before and swigged from it with a grimace.

The dawn light glowed like a vein of pink quartz as the sun crept over the landscape. They had chosen a small clearing off the weather-beaten track from Stonetree, the town they had ridden from as heroes, now miles distant. Here, the rough scrub had given way to darker desert, sands red as rust and ochre pillars of rock cut into flat-topped mesas by hundreds of years of wind. The rising sun cast shafts of light through the low clouds, illuminating a cluster of bluffs in the middle distance made of black volcanic rock. Fivehawk studied them grimly.

"The Burnt Hills," said Tyler, stepping up to his shoulder. "Guess that's why they got that name. Looks like the ground after a forest fire, or something."

The Indian removed a crumpled square of paper from his buckskin jacket and unfolded it; a crude map, hastily drawn, it showed the location of a played-out copper mine nestled at the edge of the black foothills. "Not far now."

Tyler drained the last of his coffee from its tin mug and kicked out the embers of the campfire. "You think Drache is there?"

Fivehawk tensed at the mention of the name. They had already crossed paths once with Robur Drache and his outriders, when the ruthless rail baron had attempted to abduct the entire population of Stonetree, and in the process they had come face-to-face with his evil. Tyler had been searching for his uncle and found only anguish at arriving too late to rescue him. Fivehawk had ridden to the town on the trail of his own family – his lost sister. Together they had fought off Drache's men, but the cost had challenged each of them to their very soul. Brought up in the ways of the People, Fivehawk had always understood that the world had a hidden, secret counterpart where forces of light and dark kept each other in check, but he had never considered that he might one day be part of that fight – and Tyler, poor, foolish Tyler, had discovered that his clear-cut view of things failed to include the lurking evil of Drache's poisoned soul. The man – if he still could truly be called that – was a force of death and corruption, reaching out across the West in service to an elemental malignancy that the People only whispered of in legend. The Faceless.

"Hey, Fivehawk?" Tyler nudged him. "You kinda drifted off there for a second. You OK?"

"I was just thinking. Drache knows of us now. He will be waiting."

Tyler busied himself with his gunbelt. "That's true, but what choice do we have?" He pointed at the hills. "There's a mine down there with God knows how many innocent people slaving to dig up that same kinda weird rock we found in Stonetree, all because that snake wants it. My Uncle Bill is in there, and maybe your sister too. You telling me you're afraid to go in there?"

Fivehawk shook his head. "No, but we must be careful. We cannot just ride into the camp and call him out."

Tyler drew his Peacemaker revolver in a flash and spun it around his finger, then flicked it back into its holster. "No? That's just what I aim to do."

Folding the map, Fivehawk moved to his horse, comforting the chestnut stallion. "Then you will die, Tyler," he said coldly. "Did you forget fighting his outriders? Do you not recall unloading your gun into Drache's henchman, Rook, only to have him walk away?"

"He bled green blood. That's not a thing a man forgets real quickly."

"Then you also remember that we only stopped him with the sky rock—"

"Oh yeah. The magic stone."

Fivehawk's face hardened. "We cannot kill Drache. Not here. Not now. Not yet."

Tyler exploded with sudden anger. "Why the hell not? He took everything that means anything to me, stole it right out from under my nose! Just give me one shot and I'll end his miserable life right here!"

"You cannot kill a demon with human weapons!" Fivehawk retorted.

"Oh, I forgot. Your redskin legends with their prophecy and all. Boojum demons and monsters falling out of the sky." Tyler sneered. "Listen, I may have seen some right peculiar things since I hooked up with you, but that don't mean I buy your mumbo-jumbo."

The Indian fumed inwardly. "What you believe does not matter! Even a pig-headed paleface like you must admit that facing him now would be suicide!"

Tyler opened his mouth to protest, then closed it and kicked angrily at a stone. "Ah, heck. I know you're right, but I'm just so riled I can't think straight!"

"I will consider that an apology, then," Fivehawk allowed. "We must approach the mine by stealth, in silence like the eagle. We must seek help to liberate the slave workers, and only then can we continue our hunt for Drache and his minions."

"We could rally the prisoners," Tyler considered.

"Indeed. And there may be others we can call on," Fivehawk added, his eyes searching the ridges of the mesas. *Guide me, Old Grandfather*, he thought to himself, remembering the sightless shaman who had started him on his journey, *Help me to defeat this evil.*

Unseen by either of them, a nearby boulder trembled slightly and appeared to shift, a small human shape the colour of the rock suddenly emerging from its surface. Silently, the stone-skinned figure dropped to the ground and vanished into the shadows.

Fivehawk tensed and turned, a warning in his eyes.

"What is it?" Tyler asked, his hand dropping to his pistol. "Someone coming?"

"It's nothing," said the Indian, after a long moment.

They rode as close as they dared before leaving the horses hidden in the lee of a huge fallen boulder, then picked their way around the rocks to a ridge that provided a vantage point over the Burnt Hills mine.

"Doesn't look played-out to me." Tyler grimaced.

The mine compound was a mixture of prison camp and workhouse, ringed by the black bluffs of the Burnt Hills themselves. Only two paths were marked through the hills, one a dusty trail that snaked away into the desert, the other a long stretch of rusted railroad track that disappeared behind the tallest of the dark foothills. Fivehawk started when he noticed a sinister iron shape at the railhead.

"Look there. Drache's personal railway engine."

Tyler nodded. "What did they call that thing? The Black Train?" Reaching into his trail-coat, the gunslinger removed a slim cylinder and twisted it in his hands. "It's a telescope," he explained. "Used to belong to my uncle when he was a soldier in the war."

Fivehawk took the spyglass and studied the train through it. The huge machine sat at idle on the rails like a resting metallic dragon, thin plumes of grey smoke issuing from its funnel. Behind the engine, four carriages of similar design were arranged, with shuttered windows and featureless flanks. The Indian spotted what had to be two of Drache's outriders, clad in voluminous duster coats and flat preacher hats, prowling the length of the train with rifles slung over their shoulders. "If the train is here, then so is Drache." He handed the telescope back to Tyler, who surveyed the rest of the compound.

"I see plenty of barracks, looks like..." he said aloud. A dozen clapboard buildings were arranged in a square close to the mine entrance, and through the lenses Tyler saw ragged men and weary women catching a moment's rest in the shade or else shuffling dejectedly towards the mine. He tried to keep his hands from trembling, afraid that the next face he might see would be his uncle's; the chilly fear in his chest threatened to overwhelm him.

Even with the naked eye, Fivehawk could see the pattern of the mine's operations. Fresh groups of workers were being marched into the mouth of the mine while others emerged blinking from the darkness, pushing iron hand-carts loaded high with cargoes of rock. The rocks were deposited in a corral, where more slaves appeared to be sorting through them, discarding many and placing the remainder in a hopper. "That large shack, at the north end," he whispered. "They must be digging out the sky rock fragments in there."

Tyler turned his telescope on the ruddy-coloured barn. "What makes you so sure?"

"There are no outriders nearby. Remember, the stone is like poison to them—"

"Which is why they have to use slave labour to mine it. Clever." Tyler paused, searching the compound once again. "There, by the railhead. A whole lotta those filthy jaspers standing right there."

Fivehawk followed Tyler's lead to another cluster of huts, with a stable nearby. Even at this distance, the wind carried the sound of rough laughter and harsh voices to the ridge from the gathering of outriders near the central well. Tyler cursed under his breath as he watched a huge thug with a shiny pig-ring through his nose extend a foot and trip a passing slavegirl. The woman dropped to her knees, spilling a bucket of water on the ground.

"Pick on someone your own size, fatso," he hissed to himself.

Fivehawk rolled on to his back, below the line of the ridge. "This will be more difficult than I thought. There are guard towers at all points of the compass, most likely with sharpshooters on watch, and fences around the camp."

Tyler took a moment to study the enclosure. The barbed wire barrier seemed to waver in the wind, like tall grass. "Almost like it's alive, somehow..." he mumbled.

"We must find another way in," Fivehawk continued. "Perhaps by night?"

Tyler lowered the telescope. "The front door."

"You are a fool if you think you—"

"Just hear me out," Tyler snapped. "You're always telling me I got a mouth as quick as my gun, well I reckon here's how I can use it."

"Go on."

"Looky here." He handed the Indian the spyglass once more. "See those wagons off by the barns, near the well? I figure this place has to have supplies brought in from outside, right? If I could find a wagon on its way in, I could hop a ride along, so to speak."

"And you think you could talk us out of trouble if we were caught?" Fivehawk raised an eyebrow.

"Uh-uh. I said me, not us."

Fivehawk remained unconvinced. "Why must you

constantly try to get in harm's way, Tyler? You are rash like the hare, not clever like the—"

Tyler waved a hand in front of his face. "Spare me the animal stories! I can do this, trust me." He paused. "Once I'm in, I'll figure out the lay of the land, see if I can get a little resistance going on, or something, and maybe you can come up with some reinforcements."

Fivehawk studied the gunslinger, reading the need in his eyes. Although he held it in check, Tyler feared for his uncle's life and would be willing to risk his own just to see him. It was an emotion the Indian understood all too well, and he nodded assent. "Very well. But you must be careful. The outriders will kill you where you stand if you are recognized."

"Now, what about you? You said something about there being others who could help us?"

Fivehawk lowered his eyes. "Perhaps. There is a story of a tribe that lives near here — we call them the Hidden People. If I can find them, they may be able to aid us against the demons. I can petition the tribal elder for braves to help us against the outriders."

"You don't sound like you're too sure they'll say yes," Tyler drawled, turning to the telescope once again.

Fivehawk frowned. "They're not called the Hidden People for nothing. No one has seen them in a hundred years, and no white man has ever laid eyes on them."

Tyler swore under his breath, his attention elsewhere. "Gotcha, you snake!"

"What do you see?" asked Fivehawk.

"Take a look," Tyler replied, handing him the spyglass.

At the blunt prow of the Black Train stood the unmistakable apparition that was Robur Drache; his bullet-shaped bald head shone in the sunlight, accenting the tinted glasses balanced on his nose and the single silver ring through his ear. To his left stood a woman clad in black leather with hair the colour of fire, and a tall, gangly man who played with a coiled whip. Drache's voice was lost on the wind, but his gestures were clear enough, harsh and angry.

And Fivehawk's heart leapt into his mouth when Drache looked up and stared him straight in the eye.

2: NO WAY OUT

Drache stopped speaking in mid-sentence, gazing up past Ox's flabby face to the ridgeline overlooking the mine. The outrider blinked, and nervously scratched at the ring though his nose. At his side, Rattler licked his lips and attempted to maintain a little composure.

"Ah, sir?" he lisped. "You were saying?"

The hint of a smile curled up at the corner of Drache's lips and he looked back at his two lackeys. "It is nothing," he said with the wave of a hand, "I thought I saw a wild animal." For a moment, amusement crinkled his face, but then his earlier anger returned and he stepped up to Ox and backhanded him across the cheek.

"You are as sloppy as you are ugly!" Drache snarled. "I expected you to gather twice as much stone from the mine as you have, and you have failed me!"

Rattler cleared his throat. "Ah, Master Drache, there was a cave-in and—"

Drache's meaty hand whipped upward and caught

Rattler's throat, ending his words with a strangled hiss. "Excuses. I loathe excuses. I gave you a little responsibility, my dear Rattler, and you wasted it!"

The outrider's eyes began to roll backwards into his head.

The rail baron held him a moment longer and then released his grip, letting his minion drop to the dirt like a sack of sand. Drache turned on his heel, straightening the cuffs on his grey suit as he did. "Targa, Trebuchet," he said carefully, addressing the redheaded woman and the taller man, "come with me."

Drache strode away towards a ramshackle hut sporting a sign that read "Office", without looking back.

Targa paused as she passed Rattler, who was struggling to get to his feet. She made no move to help him. "Robur is very disappointed in you," she said silkily. Rattler hissed like his namesake, but said nothing more.

The tension oozed out of Fivehawk and he relaxed a little, uncoiling like a tightly wound spring. He licked his lips and blew out a breath.

"Did he see you?" whispered Tyler. "I swear, he looked right at you!"

Fivehawk's eyes narrowed. "And yet he did not raise the alarm. Curious."

Tyler watched Targa and Trebuchet follow Drache

towards the rickety shack. "I don't know, Fivehawk. He could be setting us up, trying to draw us in for a trap."

The Indian gave a rare half-smile. "You forget, Tyler. They already know we're coming after them, so of course it's a trap. We just have to spring it on them, not the other way around."

"I guess." Tyler turned around and used his telescope to survey the rocky wilderness around them, following the trail from the mine entrance out to where it intersected the path they had ridden from Stonetree. In the distance, a comma of dust was approaching, kicked up from the wheels of an advancing wagon. "No time like the present, I suppose."

Fivehawk squinted. "I see it too." He paused. "You really think this plan of yours can work?"

"Sure." Tyler collapsed the spyglass and got to his feet. "We ambush this guy and bag him, then I sneak in. Piece of cake." The Indian said nothing, a sceptical look on his face. "What, do you think I'm making this up as I go along?"

"Yes," said Fivehawk. "I do."

Tyler scowled and set off down the ridge, towards the trail.

The office was dilapidated, its floorboards missing in places, and the roof patched with sackcloth. Wide fans of white cobweb decorated the corners, inhabited by fat, watchful spiders. With a playful glint in her eyes, Targa delicately plucked one of the arachnids from its home and ran it along her fingers.

Drache tapped his black glasses and growled. "This will not do. This will not do at all." He studied a torn map pinned to one wall. "Our benefactor has made certain demands of me that Rattler has fallen short on, and now we must make up for lost time."

Trebuchet rolled his bullwhip between his fingers. "Shall I make an example of him, *Monsieur*? A thousand lashes should suffice."

Drache waved him away. "No, no. Later perhaps. It is leadership, you see, that is the failure here. I granted him the chance for superiority and he came up wanting."

Targa let the spider return to its nest and looked around the room, an expression of faint disgust on her face. "Master, perchance I could suggest that better leadership would motivate the workers here. Like Mister Trebuchet, perhaps?"

The Frenchman's eyes narrowed. He no more wanted to be left in this desolate dusthole than Targa did, and resentment flared in him. "I—" he began.

"My thoughts exactly!" Drache interrupted. He nodded to Trebuchet. "I need someone I can trust to run this mine, to find me what our benefactor seeks and find it quickly!"

"The stone," Targa added, her mouth tightening as she recalled the agony that the glowing sky rock

18

caused her. She always dismissed science as a tedious waste of time, something for dull little men in white coats who peered at tubes of foul liquid, and yet she also wished that she could understand the rational reason why the rock's mere presence in a room would make her double up in pain. Drache had told her once that the benefits their unseen benefactor gave her were, like all things, offset with deficits, and that the sky rock was just that. Every minion who became Drache's vassal would suffer the same, while those outside his influence were immune. It was a small price to pay, she reasoned, but yet being so close to a mineshaft full of the damnable stone made her tense and uncomfortable.

Drache was speaking again, warming to his subject. "Not just that poisonous stone, my dearest Targa. There is more here than just that, and that is why I need my best followers to take control." He nodded to the Frenchman. "You, Trebuchet."

Trebuchet's knuckles whitened around the whip he held and he nodded curtly, eyeing Targa's small smile of victory – but her triumph lasted only a moment.

Drache turned to face her. "And you, Targa. Both of you."

The woman covered her surprise well, and now it was Trebuchet's turn to gloat. "We live to serve, Master Drache," he said carefully.

Drache reached up a hand to stroke Targa's red

hair. "Ah, my dear, do not be disheartened. I am giving you an opportunity to please me and earn my gratitude."

"I will double the shifts recovering the stone," Trebuchet said. "We will see the mine empty of it, even if we have to work the slaves to death."

"Excellent!" Drache clapped his hands. "Once we have all the sky rock, we'll destroy it and rid ourselves of this poison for ever. But that is not your only task here, my minions. Our benefactor has an additional task for you, something foolish Rattler and his outriders cannot be trusted with."

"We live to serve," said Targa, echoing Trebuchet with venom in her voice.

"I know you do." He paused, massaging his temples, as if recalling some painful experience. "Our ... benefactor was most insistent." Drache managed. "A jewel was lost here in the past, a sphere the size of an apple, made of sapphire."

Targa's eyes flashed. "Sapphire?" she repeated. "How lovely."

"It is very important that you find it and bring it to me." The baron's voice took on a warning tone. "I must possess it, understand?"

"Your will is our command." Trebuchet smiled. "It shall be found."

"I know it will. I have a man here at the camp, an oily tick by the name of Leadbelly. He has a laboratory out by the mine entrance in which I allow him to conduct research in return for certain of his skills. Motivate him, Trebuchet, motivate him to locate that jewel and dig it up. Its value is ... well, beyond your comprehension."

The Frenchman's eyes narrowed at the veiled insult. "Indeed, sir?"

Targa gave an acidic smile, enjoying Trebuchet's irritation, and Drache nodded to her, as if he were pleased with her performance.

He pulled a pocket-watch from its fob into his hand. "Good, good. You will not fail me." He snapped open the cover. "You would not dare to."

Targa fought down a jolt of fear with a smile, watching her reflection in Drache's dark spectacles. "You have an appointment?"

"Time. Time is against us, my minions. I have business to attend to." The rail-baron snapped the watch shut and left them behind, each cursing the other and the turn of events that had left them there.

Fivehawk's eye for the lie of the land found them the perfect spot for an ambush, just shy of the edge of the black scrubland of the Burnt Hills. Tyler weighed his Peacemaker in one hand and chewed his lip.

"We're not going to be able to shoot this guy, that's for sure. The wind'll carry any shots to the mine, and Drache's outriders will come looking. You got any magic stuff in that bag of yours to whack him with?"

Fivehawk shook his head, one hand resting lightly on the leather pouch around his neck. "Nothing to 'whack' people with, no. My medicine bundle is not a weapon."

The wagon was drawing closer; a single horse tugging a large load at a sluggish pace through the shifting dust.

Tyler rubbed his chin. "I guess we have to do it the old-fashioned way, then." Stepping out from behind the cover of some brush, the gunslinger walked to the middle of the trail and dropped, face-first, into a sprawl across the path.

Fivehawk cringed. *Great Spirit*, he said to himself, *am I doomed to spend my journey with only this reckless fool as company?*

The Black Train came to life as Drache approached, the inert metal of the massive locomotive awakening with needle-thin jets of steam. The rail-baron paused before Rattler and his knot of outriders, who fell silent. One of the slaves, a young woman, was on her knees at Ox's feet, collecting an upturned bucket.

"What happened here?" Drache asked mildly.

Ox looked on blankly, his mouth open. One of the other outriders, a pale fellow with crooked teeth, grimaced. "She tripped over again, see."

Drache extended a hand to the girl and helped her to her feet. "What is your name, child?"

"Tuh-Tulsa," she managed, a mixture of fear and defiance in her tone.

"Did you fall?"

She looked at the ground, angry and ashamed. "I guess." The pale outrider giggled to himself in a high whine.

In the next second Drache had his hand placed flat on the outrider's chest. "You are a fool," he murmured. The pale man's eyes began to bulge and he gasped, clutching at Drache's arm. Muscles and veins stood out on his neck, throbbing obscenely. "Your heart is about to stop," Drache said, as if he were a schoolteacher describing some simple event to a pupil. "You are going to die."

A strangled yelp escaped from the pale outrider and he sank to the dirt, trickles of greenish, olive-coloured blood running from his mouth, eyes and nostrils.

Tulsa's hand flew to her mouth in horror, and around her Rattler and the other outriders shifted like nervous cattle.

Drache rubbed his hands together as if wiping dirt from them. He favoured Tulsa with a smile. "There. Now, return to your duties, my dear."

The girl needed no more bidding, and fled. Rattler's eyes darted towards Ox and back, but Drache merely nodded to him.

"There will be no more petty thuggery, no more wasting of my time. Is that clear, Rattler?" The baron's tone was soft and pleasant, and it petrified the outriders all the more for it.

"Yes sir," hissed Rattler. He prodded Ox harshly. "Back to work!"

Drache smiled and mounted the train.

There was a very real moment when Tyler feared that the wagon would roll right over him without stopping, crushing him under the horse's hooves and the wooden wheels; but instead, the buckboard halted and he heard a mumbled curse followed by steady footsteps towards him.

"Eh," said a voice, and a boot-tip nudged him in the ribs. "Wake up, there." Tyler held his breath and continued to imitate a corpse, part of him hoping that the wagon driver wouldn't think of putting a few bullets in him, just to be on the safe side.

He sensed movement as the driver crouched over him. Something hard poked him in the back — a rifle barrel. "You be dead?" said the voice. "Be you? Huh?"

Tyler struggled not to laugh. *I'm supposed to be a corpse, you idiot*, he thought, *do you expect me to say yes?*

"This better not be some kinda ambush, is all I'm saying."

Tyler took his cue and rolled suddenly to his knees, his pistol appearing from where he had hidden it under his chest. "Then it just ain't your lucky day, is it?"

The driver was a buck-toothed man with skin the colour of straw and an eyepatch. He almost fell over himself in surprise. "What what what?"

"Drop the gun!" Tyler grated.

"You drop your gun!" the rider retorted, raising his rifle.

"No, you drop yours!"

"No, *you* drop *yours*!"

Stepping out from behind him, Fivehawk tapped the driver on the shoulder. As he turned, the Indian snapped a twig under his nose and he fainted, dropping to the dirt in an instant sleep. Fivehawk folded his arms and glared at Tyler. "Where did you learn that kind of ambush? In a schoolyard?"

The cowboy shrugged, brushing dust from his jacket. "It worked, didn't it? What did you give him, something like smelling salts?"

"Sleepwood," Fivehawk answered, moving to the wagon. "There's a lot of supplies here, food, rope, barrels of gunpowder." He indicated a wooden box. "Dynamite. There are chemicals as well, dozens of bottles of acid."

"The explosives will be for blasting in the mines," Tyler said. "Can't figure why Drache would want acid, though." Acting quickly, the gunslinger unhooked the black horse from the wagon and substituted it with his own brown-and-white dappled mare. "Maybe it's to destroy the rock with?"

Fivehawk searched the snoring rider, taking his

hat, coat and eyepatch. "He has a letter here." Tyler took the paper and examined it.

"It's a bill of lading, from one of Drache's warehouses. Says our sleeping beauty here is one Mister Doglin of Kansas City." He folded the paper and tried on the flat preacher hat for size. "Bye-bye Gabe Tyler, hello Mister Doglin."

The Indian tied Doglin's comatose form to the black horse and cracked its reins; spooked, the animal reared up and bolted back along its route into the desert. "He won't wake for at least a day, so you have until then to find your uncle."

Tyler put on the rider's overcoat and settled into the buckboard's seat. "And you? What happens if I need to find you, or if everything goes south on me?"

Fivehawk indicated a mesa a few miles to the west, lower and flatter than its neighbours. "There's a cave there, filled with paintings on the walls that some say the Hidden People drew. If I'm going to try to find them, it is as good a place as any to start searching."

"Suppose they want to stay hidden?"

"They won't. Once I tell them about Drache's misdeeds, they will help us to defeat him and his men. No one could stand by and let such evil take place unopposed."

"But how can you be sure they'll help us?"

"I am sure," Fivehawk replied with finality,

ignoring his own doubts. "You enter the camp under cover as this outrider and wait for me to return with the braves. Learn as much as you can about Drache's plans here and search out any weaknesses in the defences for when I come back."

"Got it."

The Indian hesitated for a moment. "Tyler, don't go off half-cocked while I'm gone with some crazy, spur-of-the-moment plan. Neither of us can handle these outriders alone."

Tyler made a hurt face. "Say, what do you think I am? Some hot-head with no patience and an itchy trigger finger?"

Fivehawk said nothing, and simply gazed levelly at the cowboy.

Tyler grunted and put on the eyepatch. "Well. Good luck, Fivehawk."

"Yes, to you as well." The Indian gave him a final nod and then urged his horse up on to the scrub, towards the mesa.

Tyler paused and blew out a breath. "Hello," he said to the air. "My name's Doglin." He shook his head, tugging on the reins. "Nah, too nice." As the wagon resumed its journey, he tried again, pitching his voice a little lower. "Ahm Doglin, y'all hear me?" Pause. "Nope, too dumb." Tyler set his face in a wild grimace. "How about – I'm Doglin, who the heck are you?!"

He rode on towards the Burnt Hills. Behind him,

a man-shape the colour of sand detached itself from a rocky outcropping and ran in silence, bare feet hardly glancing off the ground, towards the towering stone mesas.

Targa spat and hissed like a cornered wildcat. "You Gallic idiot!"

"I?" snorted Trebuchet. "You try to have me packed off in this dismal outback and then blame me when the Master forces you to tag along? You are the idiot, *cherie*, for thinking you could manipulate him!"

Her eyes flashing, Targa kicked at a chair in anger. "Damn him! I'm not some henchman like those boorish outriders, to be ordered around and commanded!"

Trebuchet shook his head and laughed. "Ah, my poor dear Targa. Are you sorry to see that you mean as little to Drache as the rest of us?" He sat, placing his boots up on the table. "You cannot control the heart of a heartless man. Your female wiles and batted eyelashes are wasted on him."

"We shall see..." Targa growled.

"He has but one desire in his life, pretty Targa. One need that subsumes all others."

Her fury spent, she sat across from the Frenchman. "That thing he communes with in his study. 'Our benefactor'."

"That object, the Instrument as he calls it, is

merely some sort of tool, a telegraph through which he takes his orders."

"I grow weary of taking *his* orders," she hissed.

"What's this?" Trebuchet smiled. "Dissension in the ranks? Surely you are not tiring of the gifts our service to Drache has given us?"

Targa lowered her voice. "Do not pretend you do not feel as I do, Frenchman. Drache wields his power while we live off the scraps from his table."

"And pitiful scraps at that."

"Now he leaves us here, surrounded by this tainted stone, most likely to choke and die on it, while he is elsewhere."

Trebuchet removed his tobacco pouch and began to roll a cigarette. Outside, a thin, unearthly whistle echoed around the hills. "That damnable train of his is on its way. We are alone now." He paused. "Perhaps we should consider this an opportunity instead of a impediment."

"What do you mean?"

"This jewel that Drache would have us find..."

Targa licked her lips. "Yes. A sapphire as big as a man's fist."

"Curb your greed for a moment and consider this. A mere gem would not interest the Master ... money has little attraction to him. This jewel must have some other value, something more alluring."

"Power." Targa nodded. "His only real weakness is his addiction to power. He craves it like opium."

Trebuchet struck a match and lit his cigarette. "Then imagine what he might give to possess it."

A slow smile spread across Targa's face like a knife emerging from a sheath.

3: VILLAGE OF STONE

Even as he approached the mesa, Fivehawk sensed that something was not right about the place. The desert wind was gentle on his face, but the usual scents of animal and plant he came to expect were strangely muted, almost as if they were concealed somehow. The wide, flat butte stood like a vast sentinel, overlooking random towers of wind-carved rock and the secret curls of canyons and gullies made by hundreds of years of winter snows and infrequent rains. Leaving his horse behind, Fivehawk shouldered his Springfield 1873 rifle and carefully picked his way to the foot of the flat-topped mountain. All across its wide vertical face were gaps that might hide watchful eyes, and he peered at them, concentrating his mind to focus his senses.

Nothing. No sound of man or beast here.

At first he thought the cave would open itself to him, reveal its location like a vein of gold glittering in the rock, but his survey of the mesa showed nothing. He chewed his lip, kicking at a loose stone and began again, slowly measuring each step around the rocky butte, eyes searching the very grains of sand themselves for a marker, some sort of indicator. As the sun tracked across the sky and into midday, Fivehawk stopped and stood still on two occasions, gripped with the thought that, if the legends were not outright fiction, then perhaps he was in completely the wrong place. He sighed. Maybe this was a sort of trial, he reasoned, the Great Spirit's way of testing his resolve and dedication? If so, he was failing at it. Fivehawk massaged his stiffening neck with one hand, thinking hard about the story told to him as a child about this place, and felt a gentle breeze on his face. He paused; there was no wind here, and yet he felt the passage of air ... how? He took a step forwards and blinked in surprise. A dark patch of shadow stood out in front of him – but not a shadow, he suddenly realized. Not a shadow at all. Fivehawk felt a curious twang of excitement in his chest. It was the mouth to the Painted Cave, tall and thin, a knife-wound in the mesa's rocky hide, in a place he'd walked past twice already. He sucked in a breath and entered.

Inside, the air took on a cooler taste. There was water nearby, he noted. Somewhere beneath his feet, an underground river flowed, sending faint trails of moisture up into the rocks. Fivehawk paused, striking a match to light a torch pulled from his bag, and then moved inward. Here, the breeze moved faster, playing tricks on the ear with indistinct whines and whistles. The passage narrowed almost to the height of a man before suddenly arching away, up towards an invisible ceiling.

Fivehawk blinked at a single shaft of sunlight that shone down from a crescent-shaped hole above him. He was in a vast open space, the walls of which were lost beyond the ring of flickering light cast by his torch. The mesa had a huge hollow at its heart. The Indian turned, stepping over a cluster of fallen rocks, and moved along the wall. After two or three steps his hand brushed against something rough on the rock face. He peered at it; a crude drawing of a man, a stick figure with a headdress of horns painted in white and ochre. The figure was pointing into the dark. Fivehawk followed its lead with the torch – and gasped.

The torch illuminated a vast mural at least a hundred yards wide that disappeared up into the darkness. He glimpsed armies of stick men in battle with each other, portrayals of buffalo hunts, lines of tepees and winding scrawls of symbols that seemed to go on for ever.

Something shimmered in the corner of his eye and Fivehawk spun on his heel, holding the burning torch out in front of him, his other hand resting on his medicine bag. He was still alone in the cavern. Fivehawk was about to relax his guard when a chilly realization made him shiver.

The pile of rocks he had stepped over to enter the vault was gone.

*   *   *

Tyler drew the wagon to a halt and gave the outrider guard at the gate what he thought was a cocky, tough nod. In reply, the guard yelled something indistinct, and the six-foot-high wooden gate opened for him. Tyler chewed his lip and guided the wagon into the mine camp, taking a sideways look at the rolls of barbed wire that flanked the gate and circled the mine. Although the wind had dropped here, the wire seemed to be twisting of its own accord, coiling and uncoiling like – well, like a snake. Tyler shook the idea from his head. He had other things to think about right now. He steered the wagon past the tip of the rusty railhead, noting that the Black Train had already departed, although the two cattle cars that had been used to transport the people kidnapped from Stonetree – including his uncle – were still there. This was a good sign then, both that Drache might not be around and that the abductees were likely to be somewhere on the campgrounds.

He watched lines of shuffling, dirty workers file past him on their way to the mine entrance, their eyes hollow and faces slack with a mixture of fear and hopelessness. In Stonetree, Tyler had encountered victims of Drache's plans, drugged into stupidity by a rare herb that Fivehawk had called Ramah, but these people were being held in thrall by something far more powerful – their own fears. Tyler suppressed a shudder and looked away. He'd make Drache pay for this injustice.

Inside the camp proper, one of Drache's outriders waved him to a halt with a fat, meaty hand. He scratched his flabby, stubble-covered face. "I be Ox. Who you be?"

Tyler drew himself up to his full height and gave Ox a hard stare with his one eye. *I gotta remember to punch a pinhole in this eyepatch to see through*, he considered.

"I be – I am Doglin. I gotcha supplies right here." He patted the wagon. He held out the bill of lading to the outrider. "Here."

Ox took the paper and held it close to his face. "What is this?"

"Can't you read?"

Ox shook his head. "Nuh." He held the paper upside down, then turned it over. "Nuh," he repeated.

A stroke of luck, Tyler thought to himself. "Well, that there says I'm to drop off this here load and then join up with the outriders, orders of Mister Drache himself."

The outrider seemed unconvinced. "Oh yeah? Well, I ain't heard o' you, Dogman."

"Doglin," corrected Tyler.

"Where you be from? Who'd you ride with afore?"

Tyler fumbled for a quick answer. "Well, uh. I rode with the Blane boys outta Brannon City, sorta, before they got shot." He struggled to recall the names of thieves and footpads he'd seen on wanted posters during his travels. "I used to be part of the Bly Gang, out of California..."

Ox nodded at that. "Uh huh. Well, you get this stuff in the storehouse over by the well and then I guess you can get yourself some chow."

Tyler smiled. "Mighty neighbourly of you, Ox."

"OK, Dogman."

"My name is –" He paused. "Oh, never mind."

Tyler dismounted and began the process of dragging the wagon's load from the buckboard to the closest of the storehouses. Inside, the wooden shack was piled high with explosives of every kind, from boxes of blasting cap to drums of gun cotton and sticks of dynamite. He pushed back his hat and gave a low whistle.

"One dropped match and this whole place will be nothing but a greasy smear."

As he returned to the wagon, Tyler found a young woman standing next to it, her face weary but with a sharp defiance in her eyes.

"Rattler told me I've gotta help you with this load." Her voice did little to hide her dejected manner.

Tyler waved her off without thinking. "No thanks, miss. I can manage," he said kindly, then hesitated. The girl eyed him. *Mistake!* he thought. *She's a slave, and I'm supposed to be one of Drache's thugs...* But yet, Tyler's own inner sense of right and wrong was too strong to force this girl to carry a heavy load; ever since he'd heard stories as a child about the black slaves held by the wealthy before the Civil War, Tyler had hated the idea of people owning people like cattle with a passion. He screwed his face into a scowl and narrowed his eyes.

"Go on, get outta here!" he growled. "I don't need no woman's help!"

She held his gaze for a moment more and then moved off. Tyler cursed himself under his breath, chastising his lack of concentration. "I am an outrider," he told himself. "A low-down good-for-nothing name of Doglin." He tried on his scowl again and sighed. He was lousy at this secret stuff; he just hoped the Indian was having better luck.

"Hello?" Fivehawk ventured, listening to the word rebound and echo through the cavern chamber. He gripped the torch tightly. "My name is –"

The shimmer moved like heat lightning from the far corner of his right eye, a rocky outcrop suddenly shifting into human shape, coming straight at him. The Indian wheeled away to dodge – whatever it was – and felt the flood of air as something swift raced past him, within inches of his face. The torch flame trembled in the wind of the passing. Fivehawk struggled to maintain his footing as it happened again, but this time there were two of them, sweeping in on him like fish through water. He tensed and pushed himself off the wall as the two shimmering figures caught him in their wake.

Fivehawk allowed himself a momentary feeling of triumph. He'd seen enough to know that it was no Guardian or other inhuman servant of The Faceless that was harrying him; their kind had a dank, graveyard stench that was absent here. Without giving them time to attack again, he reached a hand into the pocket of his buckskin coat and cupped a pinch of blasting powder in his fingers; Fivehawk had taken a handful of the volatile chemical after discovering a case of it on the hijacked wagon. Holding the torch at arm's length, he tossed the powder into the flame and looked away. The torch flared like a starburst, for one split second illuminating the entire chasm with dancing white light.

There, to his left and right, two figures hesitated in their intents, caught by the flash like faces in a photograph. Suddenly revealed, they fled, dashing into the rocks. Fivehawk gave chase. For a moment he wondered if they had actually merged *into* the stone itself until he spotted a hidden passage concealed from any casual observer. He ran on, into another corridor of rock, deeper and deeper into the mesa. Their footsteps were barely audible, odd scrapes and chitters of skin against rock as they ran before him. When they fell silent, he stopped, tension rising in his chest. Fivehawk's senses were screaming danger, and panic filled him when he took a step forward and felt nothing before him. The ground was gone.

He twisted, the torch falling from his grasp, and fell on his face. He was clinging to the edge of a ledge, and as he pulled himself back up to safety, Fivehawk saw the torch fall away into nothingness, the flame shrinking to a dot and then guttering out. The silence of those he chased had not been them stopping, he realized, but jumping! He fumbled for his pack and rummaged through its contents, but found no more torches. So be it then, darkness. He would find his way as a blind man would, by sound, smell and touch alone.

Great Spirit, guide me, he said to himself. Then, taking six paces back, Fivehawk ran with all his might and leapt into the air, the darkness roaring in his ears. For one terrible moment, Jonathan saw himself plummeting into the bottomless pit, about to be dashed to pieces on the teeth of invisible jagged rocks, but then reality hit him hard as he landed in a heap on the opposite side, the air blasting out of his lungs in a ragged wheeze.

Nursing his bruised ribs, Fivehawk struggled to his feet and blinked. At first it seemed like a trick of the eye, but a tiny chink of daylight glowed faintly before him. Carefully, he edged towards it, discovering another short curl of stone corridor. The walls glittered with veins of copper ore and painted symbols. The Indian considered putting his rifle at the ready but dismissed the idea. He had come in search of the Hidden People, not in search of conflict. Fivehawk walked on, into the daylight. After the pitch darkness of the mesa cave, his eyes felt like they had been doused in salt water as the brilliant sunshine hit him; he shielded them and squinted as his vision painfully returned. The cave emerged into a small gully with steep, unclimbable sides and dashes of greenery scattered along its length – the miniature canyon was walled in on all sides by the natural landscape, a place that would be invisible to everything in the outside world except the birds who flew overhead. A secret place. A hidden place.

And a dozen of its Hidden People surrounded him, with spears and bows held mere inches from his chest. Fivehawk blinked and managed a weak smile.

They said nothing, wordlessly directing him into the canyon with the tips of their spears. Fivehawk opened his mouth to speak and felt a sharp point dig into the small of his back; he remained silent after that, letting them prod him towards the flat strip of grass. He carefully studied them, without making an obvious show of it. Their clothing was homespun and simple, their weapons made from flints and cut branches; this tribe had not likely changed their ways in hundreds of years. Still, the signs of the outside world were visible here and there – Fivehawk glimpsed the hilt of a buck knife in one brave's belt, and another, who stared at him with hatred in his eyes, had an aged single-action pistol in his hand. The thing Fivehawk noticed the most was their skin; it had a warm sheen to it, like wet leather, a little darker than his own. Although undecorated with war paint, each of them wore complex necklaces of twine with bone and copper shards arranged along them. They brought him to a halt and paused as a slender woman approached from another hidden entrance to the canyon. Like the brave with the pistol, she had a thin film of reddish-orange dust on her skin that made her body match the colour of the rocks.

Fivehawk gave a slight nod to himself. Perhaps that was how these people were able to mask themselves so well, by camouflaging themselves against the stony landscape. The woman halted in front of him, glancing to the other brave. She seemed a little younger than Fivehawk, no more then twenty summers by his estimation. Still no one spoke. He turned over the stories of the Hidden People in his mind – perhaps the tales had failed to mention that they were all mutes?

An unspoken communication passed between the woman and the brave with the gun; clearly she had some form of seniority in this place, considering how the others stood aside for her approach. She looked Fivehawk in the eyes; he saw concern warring with curiosity there.

"What is your nation?" she asked. Her voice was soft and melodic.

Fivehawk hesitated, the question catching him by surprise.

"Answer!" hissed the brave.

"I am Ulanutani," Fivehawk replied. The woman's eyes narrowed and the brave made a derisive noise.

"He lies. We should kill this intruder."

"That is not your decision to make, Looks-Far. The Elder must hear of this."

"I come to the Hidden People in peace," began Fivehawk, "I hold no malice or guile towards your tribe."

The woman studied him. "I believe you."

Looks-Far spat. "You cannot trust this man, Rivercloud. The laws say that intruders—"

Rivercloud held up a hand to silence him; clearly, she had more than just respect from Looks-Far and the other braves. "We know of the Ulanutani, the Wanderer Tribe. Perhaps only one of them could find our mesa, perhaps you are of their nation. You must face the Elder."

Fivehawk nodded. "I wish to. I have come to speak with him."

"Then follow me." The armed braves lowered their weapons as Rivercloud led him deeper into the canyon, but Looks-Far kept a close pace with them, his pistol always close to hand.

Rivercloud took them through another adjoining tunnel and cave where the smell of water ran stronger, and then out into the sunlight again.

Fivehawk blinked the darkness away once more and was struck dumb by the sight that met his eyes. They had entered along the rim of another box canyon, walled on all sides like the strip of green by the mesa, but this ravine was a broad valley several times larger. A scattering of trees and bushes gathered around a stream that cut across one shaded corner, and towards the furthest end he could spy a cluster of animal pens and a corral. But what stopped him in his tracks were the walls; there were no tepees or tents here for living in, but instead slots and holes carved in the living bowl of rock that formed the valley, shelves of stone interconnected by rough-hewn ladders and ropes.

"Few outsiders have ever seen our village," Rivercloud noted.

"But I – I thought the –" Fivehawk gestured back at the canyon they had just left.

"You thought that was our home?" Looks-Far laughed. "That's just a place for planting and ambushes!"

"This is our secret land, Ulanutani Wanderer." Rivercloud smiled. "Granted to us by the Great Spirit."

They descended from the canyon ridge by a well-worn path, passing dents in the rock that revealed other caverns and hollows. Fivehawk peered back along their route and examined the lie of the land. From this angle he noticed subtle elements in the geography of the place that would serve to obscure the valley from outside observers, while making it easy for those within to see invaders approaching. A simple place to leave, he realized, but a very hard one to enter.

They approached a large entrance in the rock decorated with coloured stones and symbols. Looks-Far hesitated at the threshold, but Rivercloud entered without delay, opening the blanket across the doorway and bidding Fivehawk to enter.

Inside, a full-figured man looked up to study them. A smile briefly crossed his face as he saw Rivercloud, but vanished as he saw Fivehawk – an intruder.

"Father," she began, and Fivehawk suddenly understood why she had been shown such deference, "a Wanderer has discovered us. He says he comes in search of you."

The Elder raised an eyebrow? "A Wanderer? You are of the Ulanutani nation?"

"I am Fivehawk, son of Elk's Brother. I have come to speak with you, Elder."

"He is an intruder, Elder Grey Arrow," growled Looks-Far. "The pit still has much room in it. We should throw him in, not listen to his lies."

Grey Arrow paused, mulling over his thoughts, while Fivehawk sweated. Finally, he spoke again. "Only the Ulanutani would know of the Painted Cave, and they would not speak of it to others – but

44

has your path brought you here to live or die? That is the question we must seek an answer to."

Looks-Far smiled thinly, glancing between Fivehawk and Rivercloud; with sudden clarity, Jonathan noticed an edge of tension that connected them.

"Our home will be yours for the moment, Fivehawk," said Grey Arrow carefully. "My daughter will see you have food. Then we will talk of paths."

"Thank you, Elder," Fivehawk replied after a moment. He desperately wanted to speak to Grey Arrow immediately, but to refuse his hospitality would be to ignore the traditional ways and invite the Elder's displeasure; if he were to request the Hidden People's help in his mission, he would need Grey Arrow's goodwill. He nodded and followed Rivercloud from the Elder's chamber.

Looks-Far knelt at Grey Arrow's side. "What is this madness? Our sacred way is to protect our charge from all outsiders, and yet we allow this brave to enter unopposed?"

"You forget your place, Looks-Far," the Elder admonished mildly. "My son-in-law to be should watch his tongue." Grey Arrow paused. "Are you angry at this Fivehawk because he got past you into the caverns, or because he turns my daughter's head?"

Looks-Far's gaze dropped to the floor and he said nothing.

Grey Arrow nodded. "Rivercloud has always been interested in the tales of the Wanderers, nothing more. If he has come here, it is because the Great Spirit wishes it. But he will not stay. It is not the way of his tribe."

"And if he does wish to remain? Or if he has come seeking more than just an audience with you?" Looks-Far gestured towards a tunnel entrance to the rear of the Elder's chamber, barred by a wooden door.

Grey Arrow's pleasant face hardened. "Then there is always the pit."

4: SNAKEPIT

Targa made a show of yawning like a cat, rolling her eyes in mock boredom. Trebuchet snorted at her and returned to the business at hand. Drache's lieutenants had entered the shabby hut at the mouth of the mine to find it empty. Targa gave the sign above the door – "Laboratory" – an arch look but said nothing. Within, the hut was an exercise in controlled chaos. At first, Trebuchet had thought a tornado might have whipped through the interior leaving papers strewn everywhere and snarls of glass pipe wound around retort stands, but it was clear that whoever worked here had a mind that neglected even simple cleaning tasks in favour of study.

Targa wandered along racks of chemicals in glass carboys and test tubes, running her fingers along them, her nails tick-tick-ticking as they clicked over them. Some benches sported jars of formaldehyde with obscene, fleshy things inside, pickled organs and other malformed objects that made her face pinch in disgust. Trebuchet used the butt of his bullwhip to poke through random piles of paperwork, looking at meaningless scrawls of longhand writing and pencil sketches that seemed more like the work of a child than a scientist.

Targa tapped a blackboard that stood by the far wall. "What is all this?"

Trebuchet turned to see; the board was filled with a scribble of text where only one word in ten appeared to actually be in English. Oddly shaped glyphs were clustered in one corner, and at the centre was a diagram of a faceted ball, shaded blue.

"The jewel?" Targa wondered, brushing hair from her face. "Delightful."

The door banged open behind them to admit a portly, florid-faced man who peered owlishly at them through wire-rimmed spectacles the size of dimes. In his hands he carried a dozen rolled-up maps, a leather sample case and a surveyor's tripod. He made an angry whining noise when he saw them.

"Stop that this instant! Get out! Get out of my laboratory!"

Trebuchet gestured with his whip. "Mister Leadbelly, I presume?"

"Doctor Leadbelly!" corrected the man with a squeal. "What are you doing? Don't touch what you don't understand!"

Targa made a face and began to toy with a piece of chalk, sketching spider-web designs over the blackboard's contents.

"We have not met, Doctor. I am Trebuchet, and

this charming young lady is Targa. Mister Drache, your employer, sent us here? Perhaps you've heard of us?"

Colour drained from Leadbelly's face and he dumped his load on a nearby bench. "Yes, of course," he managed, his anger fleeing, and replaced by anxiety. "How silly of me to be so rude."

Trebuchet carefully moved a pile of papers from the seat of a stool and sat. "We've come to check on the progress of your work."

Targa tut-tutted. "Ask the dreary little man where the jewel is."

"In time, *cherie*. Doctor, your progress?"

Leadbelly broke into a broad grin. "Yes, of course," he repeated. "You've come at a most auspicious moment – I think I may have made a breakthrough."

"What do you mean?"

"The paintings and the glyphs are of course only crude representations, but I consider that together with the materials recovered from the mine and the first mound we opened—" Leadbelly broke off when a stick of chalk careened off his head.

Targa brushed chalk dust from her hands. "You irritating little twerp! You're not talking to your test tubes now! What are you wittering on about?"

Leadbelly adjusted his glasses. "Surely Master Drache has communicated the contents of my reports to you?"

Trebuchet and Targa exchanged glances. "Indulge us," said the Frenchman.

The scientist shrugged. "I have just discovered an Indian marker in one of the caves near the mine with a partial mural on one wall. It depicts the jewel." He unfurled one of the maps and stabbed at a location on it with a forefinger. "Here."

"Marker?" yawned Targa.

"Yes," gulped Leadbelly. "A series of crude pictographs painted in molten copper and dyes … pictures that provide a partial guide, uhh, a map as it were."

"Go on," urged Trebuchet, his interest growing.

Leadbelly continued. "Along with the glyphs from the chamber in the mine and the other Indian wards around the entrance, I have been able to piece together the location of a second marker, in a shallow pit a short distance from the mine. From there, we may be able to deduce the current resting place of the jewel." He licked his lips. "Now the new shipment of explosives has arrived, we'll be able to blast our way to the next marker, and finally I'll have something worthy to put in my report!"

"You mean to say that all this time you've been digging in the wrong place?" Targa asked with a sneer. "The jewel's not even in the mine?"

Leadbelly seemed nonplussed. "I had not wanted to venture a guess before, but now I am sure. Only the stone and the chamber are in the mine."

"The chamber," repeated Trebuchet.

"Yes, where the unusual rock was discovered." Leadbelly indicated a metal box close to where Targa stood. "I have samples of it in there."

Targa gave the box a repellent look and edged away from it.

Leadbelly pulled out another map sheet from under a pile of file cards, tipping them to the floor. "Here's a diagram of it."

Trebuchet studied the plan. It showed a cut-away view of the Burnt Hills and the paths of the tunnels that ranged below it, the location of the nearby underground river and the point where the veins of copper ore had been mined out. At the very deepest level, Leadbelly had drawn in a breach in the rock and an oval cavity.

"This is it?"

"It was found by a prospector named McAlpine. He was surveying the mine and accidentally set off a blasting charge that blew open the wall of the chamber." Leadbelly smiled. "It's quite remarkable, you know."

"You can't go down there," Targa scoffed. "The stone would drive you mad."

The scientist nodded. "Ah yes, the energetic power of that unusual rock. It's quite queer, the manner in which it causes pain —" he stopped, catching himself before he began to ramble on again. "I do have a way in which one can resist the effects of the stone, at least for a short time."

Trebuchet raised an eyebrow. "Do tell, Doctor."

Leadbelly pulled a bottle from one of the racks. "A preventative solution, once ingested, which provides momentary protection from the stone's deleterious nature."

"For how long?" demanded Targa.

"A few minutes, perhaps less. My attempts to make a stronger dosage have proven to be toxic. Fatally toxic."

Trebuchet took the bottle from Leadbelly and sniffed at the contents; he recoiled in anger. "You're trying to trick us!" He grabbed the portly man by his collar. "I smell Ramah in this! One swig of your potion and we would be under your control!"

"No, no, you misunderstand!" Leadbelly shrieked. "I use only enough to deaden the nerves, to protect from the pain. It has no side-effects!"

"You've tried this?" Targa asked.

Leadbelly nodded wildly. "Yes, of course. On myself."

Trebuchet scowled and released him. "Then perhaps we should see this chamber, eh?" He waved at Leadbelly. "Wait outside for a moment, Doctor."

When the scientist had left, he turned to face Targa. "What do you think?"

She shrugged. "I dislike clever men. He fears us, but he may also think he can outwit us."

"That is of no importance now, as long as we keep him from reporting to Drache, keep him believing we're following the Master's orders. If we take his philtre, we can see this 'chamber' for ourselves."

"But the jewel isn't there, you fool!"

Trebuchet smiled thinly. "Of course it isn't, my dear Targa. But clearly there is more to this mine than just the jewel. If Drache has this fat buffoon grubbing in the dirt for it, this chamber must contain something of even greater value ... and if Drache wants it, I want it first!"

Targa snorted and folded her arms. "What could possibly be found in a played-out copper mine, except rocks, rocks and more damnable rocks?"

"Why, isn't it obvious, *cherie*?" he broke into a grin, pure greed sparkling in his eyes like stolen diamonds. "Buried treasure!"

Tyler's stop at the chow tent was brief; the food the outriders ate was enough to turn his stomach into a knot. Greasy hunks of meat, half-cooked or raw, sat on tin plates with heaps of cold beans, and fat flies buzzing between them. Coughing, he took a mouthful of water from the nearby barrel and chewed on some beef jerky he'd secreted in a pocket instead. Ox waved a stinky shard of pig-flesh under his nose.

"Wahnt sum?" The fat outrider spat out flecks of meat and spittle as he spoke.

Tyler shook his head and swallowed hard, holding down the bile in his stomach. He glanced around as he stepped back out of the tent. Most of the outriders were eating, which left him ample time to take a look around the camp without fear of challenge. Slightly shifting his eyepatch – which now sported a pinhole to see through – Tyler wandered off towards the slave quarters. He ducked behind an outhouse to dodge Rattler as the outrider boss stalked past him, deep in conversation with Coaler, the dark-skinned man Tyler had glimpsed on his way into the camp. He caught a fragment of their words as they passed him.

"– gotta make it up to the Master before he comes back," Rattler was saying.

"Two days," rumbled Coaler. "Tall order."

Tyler mulled over this new piece of information. He would have to act fast, then, to find Uncle Bill and bust this mine wide open by tomorrow night at the latest. He resumed his slow walk, his mind racing. In here, he would have no clue about Fivehawk's success or failure in finding the Hidden People, and he couldn't stand by and wait for the Indian to come to him. For a brief moment, Fivehawk's warning words about "going off half-cocked" echoed in his mind – and then Tyler ignored them. No, after nightfall, he would need to leave the camp and find Fivehawk. The first few vague elements of a plan began to form in his head and he smiled to himself.

"I'll be darned. Maybe for once I won't have to make things up as I go along."

Tyler stepped over the tracks for the mine cars and stopped dead. A shambling trio of men were pushing an empty iron wagon from a spur line on to the main track, aiming to guide it through the mouth of the mine and down into its depths. Two of the faces were unfamiliar to him, but the third leapt out like a beacon.

Bill Tyler, his old frame bent with effort and caked with red dust, worked at the car, shoving with all his might to send it into the darkness of the mine. His gaze swept right over his nephew without even the slightest flicker of recognition.

And why not? Gabriel thought. *He doesn't see me, he sees another stinking outrider.* Tyler fought to control the impulse to suddenly break and run to the old man, sweep him up and charge towards the gate, six-gun blazing; but then he caught sight of the other slaves around his uncle as they all filed into the mine after the car, each of them as ragged and broken as the old man. If he was going to leave here with his uncle, Tyler resolved, it would be with every other kidnap victim and abductee following along behind them.

The sound of water rushing and an angry curse

from behind him caused Tyler to wheel around. A pool of muddy water was spreading out towards his feet in a fan from an upturned bucket, and next to it in a heap was the woman from the storehouse. Tyler put on his best scowl, but the expression died when he locked eyes with her. She'd clearly tripped on an exposed rail spike, sending her bucket flying, but her anger at a simple accident had transformed instantly into fear when she realized an outrider was standing close by. Tyler was conflicted; a *real* outrider would have shouted at her, insulted her, maybe even beaten her, but he could not. He stepped through the puddle and extended a hand to her.

She eyed him warily with the look of someone that had too often been a victim and got to her feet by herself. "I don't need your help," she ventured.

"I guess not," said Tyler. He picked up the bucket and held it out to her. "What's your name?" he asked, attempting to keep a stern tone to his voice.

"Tulsa."

"That's a place, not a name."

She frowned. "What's it to you, anyhow?"

Tyler opened his mouth to reply and gaped. Three figures were approaching from the hut closest to the mine entrance, walking straight towards him and Tulsa. The shortest was a tubby man with piggy eyes and animated hands he didn't recognize, the next a tall fellow with a nasty-looking whip at his side, but the other was very familiar. A woman with hair the colour of bonfires and a form-fitting leather outfit that made her look like some black mountain cat. The last time he had seen her, she had directed a hundred drugged men, women and children to murder him. Targa looked right at him and a question appeared in her expression.

Tyler snapped away the bucket before Tulsa could take it from him; she looked at him, then at Targa, instantly aware that something was amiss.

"You!" Tyler snapped. "With me, come on!" He grabbed her arm and marched her towards the slave quarters. Tulsa said nothing, afraid to protest but confused at the same time. When they were out of Targa's line of sight, Tyler let go and blew out an exasperated breath. "Who knew she'd still be here?" he mumbled.

Tulsa studied him carefully, eyes narrowed.

"Targa, *cherie*. Are you paying attention?" Trebuchet snapped his fingers in front of her face.

She waved him away irritably. "It's nothing. Just some thug with a face I thought I knew." She shrugged. "Drache recruits so many of these dregs from every cesspool and hellhole across the nation, is it any wonder we can't keep track of them all?"

Trebuchet smiled. "I never thought outriders were your type, my dear."

Targa snorted and ignored him. "Leadbelly, show us your prize."

The portly scientist coughed. "Yes, as you wish."

They entered the pit, lighting their way with a trio of oil lamps, and Targa gave an involuntary shudder as the daylight faded away behind them. It was like passing into the gullet of some vast earthen snake, the dun-coloured walls curving up to surround them, wooden beams dancing in the flickering light. The slave workers were a pathetic bunch, shying away from Leadbelly, who seemed to enjoy his power over them. Once in a while he would snap at one of them and grin when they cowered before him.

"How many captives are in here?" Trebuchet asked.

"A hundred, two hundred give or take a few. They die with unpleasant regularity, so it's hard to be sure. Fortunately, cave-ins are rare – it's mostly the gases that foul the air or overwork that does them in. In the early days of this operation, Master Drache gave me the opportunity to alter the vassals he brought to make them more suitable, but recently his demands for increased production have put a stop to that."

"What do you mean by 'alter' them?"

Leadbelly glanced around and grabbed a worker by the scruff of his neck. "Like this."

Trebuchet studied the worker's face and recalled the jars in Leadbelly's lab. The slave had been a man once, but now his lips and nostrils had been sewn shut, and ugly rents in his neck like a fish's gills pulsed in time with his breathing. His eyes were misted. "What have you done to this poor wretch?"

The scientist chafed at his tone. "Improved upon nature. He can perform in total darkness and breathe much thinner air than you or I. The perfect miner." He sighed. "If only I might have had more time to perfect my experiments. Master Drache has been very understanding about my research."

"I'm sure he has," Targa murmured.

The tunnel branched into a T-junction, with a heavy elevator arranged at the head. Leadbelly gestured for them to enter, waving aside a group of silent workers with a mine car between them. "We'll descend to the lower levels from here."

Slamming the lift's gate closed behind him, the portly man pulled on a knotted length of cord and a bell rang. With a jerk, the open-framed elevator began to drop into the bowels of the mine workings. Faintly-lit scenes flashed past them as they passed other levels of the pit, with groups of slaves hacking at the walls with blunt picks or stacking slabs of rock into hoppers.

Targa caught the sound of running water over the clatter of the lift's passage. "There's a river here..."

Leadbelly nodded, his rotund face bobbing in the lamplight. "Yes, yes. It runs all through this part of the area, connecting up to a stream up on the surface a few miles away. There may also be an underground lake nearby as well."

Trebuchet tensed suddenly, a shooting pain stabbing into his head. He glanced at Targa, who was pressing her fingers to a throbbing vein in her temple. "Pain."

"Ah, yes, the formula," said Leadbelly tightly, fumbling in his coat pockets. "We're feeling the effects of the stone. We're quite close now."

"The potion!" snapped Targa. "Where is it?"

Leadbelly produced the glass bottle and she snatched it from him. "Just a mouthful, now..." he managed.

Targa bolted back a shot of the liquid and passed the bottle to Trebuchet, who took a more careful sip. Both of them shivered at the foul taste. "Ach, it's bitter."

The scientist greedily drank the last of the philtre and smacked his lips. "I've grown to like it, actually."

As quickly as the pain had come, it was gone, with only the brackish after-taste and a slight numbness in the throat to remind them of the medicine.

The lift stopped sharply and Leadbelly opened the gate. "We have little time. Follow me."

Targa and Trebuchet followed him into a large cavern, the ceiling held up by huge lengths of wood and the rough floor dotted with barrels of blasting powder and boxes of dynamite. Stalactites and stalagmites extended from above and below like probing fingers, and thin rivulets of water dripped constantly. Trebuchet recognized the cavern as the oval chamber he'd seen on the map. Somewhere nearby was the steady rush of the underground river.

Targa paused to study one of the slave miners before Leadbelly urged her on. A woman, older than her, was picking through fist-sized chunks of ore; some of them glittered with the green of the jade-like sky rock. Targa smiled. Leadbelly's potion worked after all.

The scientist stopped before a curious gash in the cavern wall. Rock had fallen away to reveal a mottled surface that shone dully in the lamplight. Trebuchet touched it – it was cool and smooth. "It's metal," he said aloud.

"It is." Leadbelly twitched, rubbing his eyes. "And it's hollow." He rapped on the material with his knuckles and it rang like a cathedral bell, a deep, ominous tone. "I suspect there may be an opening nearby..."

Targa felt the pain returning. "The formula is weak!"

Trebuchet nodded, screwing his eyes closed. "We've only been here a moment..."

"We must go back!" Leadbelly gasped. This time, they did not need his bidding and sprinted back to the elevator. In moments, they were ascending and breathing hard.

"It will be another hour before we can return," said the scientist. "As you can see, until I perfect the formula. I cannot excavate the chamber in person. Perhaps you could convince Master Drache to give me more time?"

Trebuchet waved him to silence. "What about the jewel? These markers you spoke of?" He was gasping for air, tasting blood in his mouth.

"The markers are Indian ceremonial sites, in tunnels near the surface. When I find the second marker, I should be able—"

"Then find it!" Trebuchet interrupted. "Find me the jewel!"

Leadbelly hesitated. "So I would be correct in assuming that you and Miss Targa will be handling Master Drache's affairs here until he returns?"

"Oh yes," Targa said silkily. "Yes indeed. He ordered that you show us the same degree of loyalty and intelligence you have always shown to him. I'm sure you will amaze both of us with your resourcefulness."

The scientist coloured slightly. "I'll do my very best."

"We know you will," said Trebuchet, glancing at Targa. "We know you will."

5: THE HEART OF THE WORLD

Fivehawk marvelled at the intricate nature of the Hidden People's dwellings, the clever way that they had been hewn from the living rock itself. The concealed valley was surprisingly lush, considering its location in the middle of an arid wasteland; he glanced up at the sky, past the walls of stone that gathered in around it. This was a good place, a rare formation of nature that made it the perfect home for a tribe of invisibles.

Rivercloud led him past small patches of plantings where other squaws and children worked, her expression a smile as her tribe looked up in awe at a new face, an outsider. She nodded to Fivehawk. "We do not have many visitors."

He thought of the pit in the cave. "I don't doubt it."

They entered a flat sandy area, like a plaza before the stone dwellings. Fivehawk noted a number of small boulders dotted randomly around the place. Rivercloud stopped and put her hands on her hips, a mock-stern look on her face.

"Children!" she snapped. "Do not be rude to our guest!"

It was all Fivehawk could do not to gape when the stones suddenly *unfolded* into boys and girls, their heads appearing from under buckskin coats the colour of the sand, faces split in mischievous smiles covered in the same dust Rivercloud sported. She clapped her hands. "Come, come. Go and play by the stream." The children whispered and pointed at Fivehawk, then broke into a run and departed.

He studied Rivercloud. "Your tribe has a gift."

She shrugged. "A talent we are all taught from our earliest days." She touched him lightly on the arm. "We lead a secret life, Fivehawk. We hide in shadow and watch the world pass us by."

"That was Looks-Far who attacked me in the cavern?"

"Yes. And me."

"You?"

Rivercloud smiled coyly. "We became as the rocks and you stepped right over us."

Fivehawk rubbed his chin. "I never saw you, never heard you."

"It is not the first time. We've followed you ever since you arrived in our territory."

His voice took on an urgent tone. "Then you know why I am here?"

"The prison of earth," she nodded. "We are to have nothing to do with it."

Rivercloud beckoned him into one of the rooms cut from the walls, to a blanket on the floor. Another squaw smiled at them and produced bowls of food and an animal skin full of water. Fivehawk ate and drank, his mind racing.

Rivercloud hesitated between bites. "Tell me of your travels, Wanderer," she said. "We have only stories of your kind."

"I don't know where to begin. I have only seen a little of the world..."

A mixture of longing and annoyance coloured her words. "It is our lot never to venture from this place." She gestured around at the stone walls. "This is our world, and we cannot leave it."

"But you sometimes wish you could?" Fivehawk ventured.

"Oh yes!" Rivercloud's eyes widened. "To see the places where snow lies on the ground all through the year, rivers as wide as our valley, mountains and seas..." She fell silent, suddenly embarrassed. "You must think I am foolish and sheltered."

"Not at all. There is great beauty in the world beyond your valley ... but this place is beautiful as well."

Rivercloud scowled. "You sound like my father."

"Is that so terrible a thing?" Grey Arrow's voice asked.

Fivehawk turned to see the Elder enter the room,

with Looks-Far at his side. The other squaw bowed and left.

"You have eaten well?" said the tribal chief.

"He feasts like a starving animal!" Rivercloud retorted.

Fivehawk studied Grey Arrow as he sat beside him; the Elder's smile did not reach his eyes. Grey Arrow did not yet trust him, and as for Looks-Far — the brave seemed on the verge of attacking him all over again. Fivehawk kept his posture neutral and unthreatening. *I must make allies of these people*, he thought.

"Forgive my daughter," Grey Arrow began, "she has much of her mother in her, and perhaps a little too much of the crow's nature."

"It is not wrong to want to see new places..." she said quietly.

"But the outside holds great danger, does it not?" The Elder looked at Fivehawk, expecting him to agree. He gave a half-nod. "Better to live as you have lived then risk the unknown."

For a moment, it seemed that Rivercloud was about to argue, but silent warnings from her father and Looks-Far muted her. Fivehawk saw that she'd clearly had this quarrel on many occasions and never won it.

"Now, Fivehawk, son of Elk's Brother. Why have you come to our land?"

He hesitated; what could he say that would sway

Grey Arrow to his side? The Elder seemed fixed and cautious in his manner, and while his daughter appeared to be willing to accept outside ideas, Fivehawk feared that Looks-Far would oppose anything he said merely to spite him. He sighed. Looks-Far clearly saw Fivehawk as a threat to his woman, and that would not help him.

What would Tyler do? He found himself wondering, and a smile tugged at the corner of his mouth. The reckless gunslinger would have probably got into a fight already. Fivehawk took a sip of water and looked Grey Arrow in the eye, hardening his resolve. He would do only what he could; tell the truth.

"Elder," he began, "you know of my people, of our ways."

Grey Arrow nodded. "You wander the Spirit Path. The shamans speak of how your forefathers once defeated a great evil, and that you roam the land in case it one day returns."

Fivehawk sucked in a breath. "We do. And that day is coming soon."

Looks-Far's face split in a sneer. "Stories for children and weak minds about monsters and demons! Pah!"

"You mean this?" said Rivercloud. "The legend of the prophecy?"

"Answer her," Grey Arrow grated.

Fivehawk nodded. "A demon fell from the sky that

not even the Great Spirit could kill. A beast that feasted on the souls of men and spread corruption across the world—"

"We have allowed a madman into our village!" Looks-Far gibed. "A lunatic!"

"The Faceless!" Fivehawk barked, his voice rising. "It lives, even as we speak!" He turned to face Looks-Far, anger in his eyes. "I have seen its hand in warped men and crooked beasts!"

Rivercloud recoiled at the name, hardly able to speak it. "Fuh-Faceless?" Her eyes darted to Grey Arrow. "Father, say it is not true. The darkest creature in the world?"

The Elder fixed Fivehawk with a hard stare. "Is it true, Wanderer? Do you come here to sow stories of terror and fear, to drag up old fables told to frighten children?"

"It is true," Fivehawk replied with absolute conviction. "On the Sacred Hoop, I swear it."

Grey Arrow dismissed Rivercloud with a wave of the hand. "Daughter, leave us now."

She hesitated. "But—"

"Go!" shouted the Elder, and she fled. He glanced at Looks-Far, who sat heavily and drew his pistol.

An abrupt sense of threat came to Fivehawk; Grey Arrow's reaction to his words had not been what he had expected.

"You should never have come here," the Elder

said. "With mere words, in just moments, you have brought fear to life in our valley!"

"But you asked me for the truth, Elder."

"Truth is a dangerous thing," Looks-Far growled. "It can be a poison."

Grey Arrow nodded. "The Hidden People live in a secret balance with the land, Fivehawk. If you claim that monsters from the old times are about encroach on us, that balance is upset."

"I do not claim, Elder—"

"Why have you done this, Wanderer?" Grey Arrow rose to his feet and Looks-Far followed suit. "Why have you come here with this tale of yours?"

"I – I need your help, Elder. The minions of the Faceless are here, in your land even now. They hold hundreds of innocents as slaves while they cut open the ground in search of the sky rock."

"The prison of earth," said Looks-Far, echoing Rivercloud's description of the mine camp.

"Yes. We must free them, stop the dark one's plans before they are complete."

"We?" asked Grey Arrow. His eyes took on a harsh glint.

Fivehawk stumbled over his words, standing. "I came to ask for braves to aid me, Elder. With your gift of concealment, the Hidden People could breach the camp. The servants of The Faceless would be defeated."

"And what of us?" snarled Looks-Far. "We would

be revealed, our secrets known! We would be hidden no longer!"

Fivehawk was speechless; he could not believe what he was hearing.

The Elder studied him gravely. "You will find no allies here, Fivehawk, son of Elk's Brother."

"Why?" The question exploded from his lips. "You know the legend of The Faceless, that the Great Spirit himself could not kill it alone! If you refuse to help me, you may doom us all!"

Grey Arrow's face became hard and rigid. "You know nothing, boy." The Elder's voice was a razor. "Ask yourself, why are we the Hidden? What do we conceal here, in this place? It is not our people who must remain unseen, but a sacred trust that, like the Ulanutani, was granted us by the Great Spirit himself in the days when the world was new."

"I do not understand," Fivehawk bit out.

"No," said Grey Arrow. "You do not." The Elder turned his back on the young man and left the room. Looks-Far moved to follow, hesitating on the threshold.

"Stay here, Fivehawk, and do not attempt to leave. Speak to no one."

"If you will not help me, I must leave. I have made a promise to another to return to the mine."

The brave shook his head. "Your promise will go unfulfilled, then. Grey Arrow will decide what will become of you."

Fivehawk watched Looks-Far walk away, his feelings conflicted. He saw him pause to share a brief conversation with Rivercloud; they were out of earshot, but their words were clearly heated ones. Looks-Far gestured sharply in his direction — no doubt warning Rivercloud to stay away from him — but the woman studied Fivehawk with clear intent in her eyes. At least one of the Hidden People believed him.

Tyler waited for nightfall before he decided to chance leaving the mine compound; despite his near run-in with that woman of Drache's, his outrider disguise had held up in the faces of the other henchmen. Tulsa, however, was a different story. She was a sharp one, to be sure, and after he abandoned her by the slave quarters, Tyler felt her questioning gaze burning into his back as he walked away. The cowboy fretted for a moment that she might raise the alarm, call in the other outriders and sell him out in return for her own escape — but he remembered the look in her eyes, defiance but not deceit. No, she would keep silent, he was sure of it.

As the sun began to sink beneath the horizon, Tyler carefully made his way to where his horse was tethered. The dappled mare was more than a little spooked, but became calmer when Tyler approached. He glanced around at the other outriders' mounts. They seemed gaunt and hollow somehow, muscle and bone showing through their skin in odd places. He shuddered. Drache's influence extended through his minions and even to these poor beasts, as if the man's mere presence was like a germ, a foul miasma that spread over every living thing it touched, tainting them. The gunslinger quietly led his horse away, watching the movements of the outrider guards on towers.

He hesitated by the barrier fence and glanced at the rolls of razor-sharp barbed wire. It undulated like creepers, a snarl of metallic vines with deadly barbs. Here and there, knots of it seemed to throb gently, as if catching a gust of wind, but the night air was still and silent. The cowboy eyed the wire nervously. It was just a fence, right? Just barbed wire, right? He stepped over an obstruction, some fallen tree branches and rips of cloth, and paused.

Tyler considered a plan of action; he would need an excuse to leave through the front gate, and the wire was too high for his horse to leap. He vaulted into the saddle, glancing around. Suddenly, Tyler's mount snickered and backed away from the wire; a thin tendril of it had begun to extend, probing out at the animal's hooves. The cowboy jerked back the reins in fright as the wire hissed over the sand towards the horse, whispering forward like a thin trickle of rainwater down a windowpane. Tyler's hand hovered over his gun, tensing. He knew that a single shot would bring the outrider guards running.

The wire's reach stopped abruptly, and it wavered in the air, twitching back and forth like a rattlesnake's tongue. It certainly wasn't the wind making it do that, he reasoned. Somehow he knew that this fence, or whatever it was, was *alive*. And worse still, it was *hungry*.

"Damn these spooks and demons!" Tyler cursed. "Just for once, I'd like to get an easy day instead of being trapped by a ... a ... fence monster!"

"Hey," a voice behind him made him turn about. Tulsa stood nearby, a lamp in her hand. "What are you doing?"

"Get outta here!" he hissed in a mock-snarl, his outrider impersonation failing miserably.

Tulsa ignored him and walked to within a hand's-length of the wire. "It don't like fire," she said, turning up the lamp's flame and waving it at the twisted snarls of filament.

Tyler marvelled as the wire made a thin, faint squeal and shrank back. A parting formed. He looked back to Tulsa.

"Go then, if you're going," she said. "Just don't leave us all here," she added, with desperation in her voice.

"Come with me," he said, on sudden impulse. "Heck, torch the whole fence and we'll bust everyone out!"

Tulsa shook her head wearily. "This is the middle of the desert — where could we go? We've got no food, no water and no horses. None of us here even know where in the world we are. We were brought in on cattle cars with no way to see out…" She seemed to shrink a little as she spoke. "Truth be told, this place would still be a prison even if they had no fences at all."

"Hasn't anyone tried to get away?"

"Some have." Tulsa gestured at the wire, towards the cluster of branches and rags Tyler had noticed earlier. Under the light of her lamp he saw the white twigs and tatters for what they really were — bones and shreds of clothing.

"The wire," she said, by way of explanation. "Sometimes it leaves leftovers."

Tyler glanced at the gap in the fence, which had slowly begun to close up again, then back to Tulsa. He dropped his disguise and gave her a smile, tapping the brim of his hat in salute.

"I'll be back." Sucking in a shuddering breath, Tyler snapped his reins and rode through the gap in the line, the wire snapping at his horse's hooves and the scent of fresh flesh.

In seconds, he had vanished into the darkening night and out of Tulsa's sight.

Fivehawk was startled out of a fitful sleep by the sounds of angry voices in the Hidden People's village. He sat up and brushed dust from his jacket, cursing himself for dozing off. He shook his head to rid it of the last fragments of fatigue and got to his feet. The voices were distinct now, and he heard Looks-Far among them.

"– kill all intruders!" one voice was saying.

Another made a snorting sound. "And what if it is another Wanderer? What then? Do we risk the wrath of the Great Spirit and kill him out of turn?"

"Be quiet, all of you!" Looks-Far growled. "If he were a Wanderer, he would not have been caught so quickly – bring him here, and wake the Ulanutani. Perhaps we can deal with two intruders this night."

Fivehawk caught the murmur of agreement among the group and dropped back to the floor, mimicking his earlier sleep. The squaw who had brought him food earlier entered and nudged him.

The Indian sat up, faking a yawn. "What is it?"

"Grey Arrow wishes to see you. Come with me."

Fivehawk made to follow her. He paused as he passed his gear in a pile on the floor – it would be an offence to carry a weapon here, and yet it seemed likely that Looks-Far was intent on taking his life. He nodded, touching the medicine bundle around his neck; he would have to rely on other means to defend himself.

Outside, an angry crowd had gathered and Fivehawk felt the taste of threat in the air, saw the tension in every face that looked at him. Even Rivercloud avoided his glance. He said nothing, breathing evenly, ready to react if the moment came.

Looks-Far stood in front of a small campfire, framed by the flickering light of the flames. "Is it not enough of an affront to our tribe that the Wanderers know of our secrets? You broke our covenant, Fivehawk!" he snarled. "You told another of the Painted Cave, you revealed us!" Grey Arrow sat close by, his face impassive.

Two braves approached, carrying a sack that twisted and writhed; muffled curses and shouts came from within. They upended the cloth bag and a figure fell out, dropping to the dirt in a crumpled heap.

"Tyler?" Fivehawk asked. "Your timing is awful."

The cowboy blinked at the Indians assembled around him and gulped. "Ah, hello?" he managed. "I was just passing through –"

Grey Arrow shook his head. "To tell another of our land is dishonour enough, Fivehawk, but to speak of it to a white man is unforgivable."

Tyler opened his mouth to protest, but Fivehawk intervened. "This is no ordinary white man, Elder. We are brothers in our crusade against The Faceless." A fearful muttering ran around the crowd. "He owes me a life debt. He is here because he feared I might be killed, and that he might never be able to honour his duty."

Grey Arrow fixed Tyler with a hard stare. "Is this the way of it, Paleface?"

Tyler gave Fivehawk a sideways glance. "Sure is, Chief. I'm here because of – well, what he said."

"We have never allowed the palefaces into our valley!" Looks-Far gritted. "We must cast him into the pit, or else he will tell all of them about us!"

"He will not!" Fivehawk shouted. "I swear it, on my tribe and the Sacred Hoop." Grey Arrow saw the steel in Fivehawk's eyes and instantly knew that the Wanderer was speaking the truth.

"Do with me as you must," Fivehawk continued, "but spare my brother Tyler."

Tyler studied the Indian, surprise on his face. Fivehawk was risking his life to save him from certain death. "Don't do this, Jonathan."

"It is done," Fivehawk replied, then turned to Grey Arrow. "Blindfold him and return him to the desert. You know as well as I that he will never be able to find the valley again, even in a hundred years of searching."

"You agree to abide by whatever fate we decide for you, Fivehawk?"

"I will."

Grey Arrow gestured to the braves. "Release the paleface!"

Like water draining from a cup, the tension in the air faded away. The braves pushed Tyler back towards the stone corridors and Fivehawk followed. Grey Arrow watched the white man disappear into the tunnel, his voice fading into murmur as he was taken away. He glanced at Looks-Far; the brave's jaw was set hard.

In the corridor, Tyler shifted in the grip of his captors. "Wait, wait!" he shouted. "I just got here! What's going on, Fivehawk? I thought you said these people were gonna help us."

Fivehawk shook his head. "I was mistaken. You were correct, Tyler, they only wish to stay hidden."

Tyler struggled with the braves holding him, his face reddening with anger. "What?! I've been in that filthy prison, man! They're killing people by inches in there, white people and Indians too! Every one of them will be dead by the time Drache gets what he wants, and these cowards would let it happen right in their back yard!" He wrestled his way out of their grips, enraged. "What kind of yellow are you?"

"They conceal themselves to protect a sacred trust," Fivehawk said carefully, the words ashen in his mouth. "I must respect their ways."

"Well, I don't give a damn about their ways! What kind of secret is worth the lives of hundreds of innocent people?"

"Do you really want to know?" Rivercloud stepped out of the darkness. She dismissed the two braves with a word and studied Tyler and Fivehawk. "Will you understand if you see it with your own eyes?"

Tyler's bluster waned a little. "Nothing is worth turning your back on another's suffering for."

Rivercloud gave a small smile and beckoned them

into a side-tunnel. "Follow me. Then you can judge for yourself."

They doubled back into the valley, emerging in Grey Arrow's chambers where Fivehawk had first been brought. The room was empty, and Rivercloud crossed to a heavy wooden door set in the far wall. She opened it to reveal another tunnel that vanished into the rock.

The passage narrowed to claustrophobic dimensions before opening out into a spherical chamber. Fivehawk and Tyler gasped as they entered; every surface in the room was covered with glittering symbols and artwork rendered in gemstones and beaten copper. A glowing blue light filled the room, spilling from an alcove on the far wall, and it pulsed like a living thing.

"When the world was young," Rivercloud said aloud, reading the text on the walls, "the Great Spirit came to our people with a gift. He asked us to keep it safe from outsiders until the day that it would be needed, so we became the Hidden People, hiding in plain sight to protect his sacred trust."

Fivehawk stepped closer to the alcove; the glow streamed from an object nestled on a metal plinth. "And this is the gift?"

Rivercloud nodded. "It is The Heart of the World. We are its guardians, to keep it safe from the evil of the outside." Fivehawk sensed doubt in her words even as she said them.

"And this is it? A rock?" Tyler growled. "You're going to let a bunch of people die because you're afraid someone's going to steal your glowing rock?"

"Tyler," Fivehawk began, "you don't understand—"

"You're damn right I don't!" He rounded on Rivercloud. "Get me outta this redskin crazy-house! I should never have expected any help from your kind!"

Fivehawk shook his head. "Tyler, this stone may be part of the—"

"I don't want to hear any more demon mumbo-jumbo from you!" Tyler shouted. "I'm going back to the camp and I'll bust those people out myself." He stalked away, to the tunnels. "You can stay here and hide in your caves for all I care!"

Fivehawk frowned and took a step after him.

Rivercloud put a hand out to stop him. "Let him go. A white man could never understand the importance of The Heart."

The Indian paused, and glanced back at the alcove. On the plinth sat a perfect blue orb, faceted like a gemstone, as big as man's fist, an unearthly, ethereal jewel.

6: TUNNEL VISION

The dull thud of the explosion echoed around the Burnt Hills like a weak clap of thunder, creating a brief jet of smoke and ash that twinkled in the pre-dawn light. A large black bird squawked in fright and shot into the air from its perch in the rocks, like a feathered missile. Leadbelly snapped his fingers in delight as Coaler gathered up the wooden plunger box and the spools of wire.

"Clean job," Coaler grunted to no one in particular.

Trebuchet rubbed his stubbled chin watchfully. "You are sure about this?"

"Absolutely," Leadbelly replied. "Come, we'll see for ourselves when the dust settles."

They walked steadily towards the hillside. Where moments earlier there had only been a crease in the hillock's flanks, now there was a rounded hole, a dark spot.

"Why do we have to be here now?" Trebuchet asked, stifling a yawn.

"Too early for you?" quipped Leadbelly, excited

by the moment. "I notice Miss Targa did not join us."

The Frenchman shrugged. "Any man trying to rouse her before sun-up would find himself without his head."

"Yes, quite. But you must understand, the savages who dug these pits used the rays of the rising sun to mark them. A torch would not illuminate the pictographs correctly, you see, and it is vital that we decode the glyphs in order to find the resting place of the jewel."

"Indians dug these?"

It was Leadbelly's turn to shrug. "I'm not really sure what tribe they are. The murals I found at the first marker had elements of Ojibwa, Seminole and Kiowa symbology, as well as some others I don't recognize..."

They had reached the newly reopened pit. Leadbelly dropped to one knee and peered into the darkness. "Just like the other one, but it seems a little deeper."

Coaler set up a rope and a stake in the dirt while Trebuchet lit a mine lamp. He glanced up at the sky; the black of night was fading into a deep blue, being chased away by the orange glow that filled the horizon.

"Ready?" asked Leadbelly, clutching a notebook to his chest. "Time is of the essence."

Trebuchet waved him away, and after a moment

they dropped into the pit. It was as if night had fallen all over again.

"There is none of that filthy stone here, yes?" Trebuchet growled.

"No, we have nothing to fear."

Trebuchet frowned, unconvinced. "Lead on."

Leadbelly paused every yard or so to make notes in his book, the scratching sound of his pencil on paper like a burrowing animal in the dimness. He gave a little squeal of delight. "I was right! I was right again! This is most exciting!"

"We will find the jewel here?" Trebuchet ventured, his hand straying to the heavy bullwhip in his belt.

"No, I don't believe so." Leadbelly paused again, turning. "Dawn is almost upon us."

"So where, then?" Trebuchet was impatient.

"The first marker was almost an accidental discovery, at the mouth of the mine," said the portly scientist. "I had deduced a rough location from Master Drache's orders, but it was only because one of the vassals fell through a sink-hole that we found it. We blew it open, like this one." He sighed. "A shame we could not have got him out first. Still, he served a purpose. I deciphered the writings, as you know, which pointed me here. And here we have a second marker." Delight crept into his voice.

"What good will it do us?"

Leadbelly puffed himself up and arched an

eyebrow, lecturing Trebuchet as if he were a particularly dim child. "The glyphs inside the first marker pit indicate a line, north to south, across the landscape. This second will indicate another, from east to west, and where the two lines intersect..."

"That's where we'll find the jewel."

"Exactly." The scientist examined his pocketwatch. "It's time."

The rising sun emerged over the lip of the pit entrance and flooded the small cave with morning light. Trebuchet's breath caught in his throat as the walls flickered in the illumination. For a brief second he thought a colony of fireflies had awoken, but the sunlight glanced off of hidden wisps of beaten copper pressed into the walls. The small cave was full of murals, rough sketches of stick figures and drawings of the local landscape. Leadbelly scribbled frantically in his book, copying what he read into its pages. After what seemed like only a few moments, the cavern began to darken once more as the sun continued its upward journey into the growing day sky.

"Do you have it? The location?"

Leadbelly slapped Trebuchet's hands away from him. "Quiet!" he whined.

Finally he paused and removed his spectacles, wiping them on his sleeve. His small, beady eyes blinked rapidly. "Most curious. A very odd narrative, indeed."

"What are you babbling about, man? Where is the jewel?"

Leadbelly gestured at the walls. "The story reveals more than I had expected. These glyphs, they both tell a tale and point the way." He started for the entrance. "I must consult my maps."

Trebuchet felt his anger growing; Targa was right about this officious little troll, that he was far too interested in his own scholarship than their plans. Leadbelly's greed was of a far different kind, for knowledge, not power, but still no less potent. He stepped outside and found the scientist on his hands and knees, peering at his notes and a map of the territory around Burnt Hills.

Leadbelly was thinking aloud. "How very intriguing. The words warn of a danger, perhaps a great power in the earth ... that a man might be granted dominion over the stones themselves? There's also a caution, that the unwise will find themselves consumed..."

Trebuchet drew his whip and gave it a casual flick, playing out only a little of its length. The thick, metallic cord shot out and coiled around Leadbelly's neck. The Frenchman gave it a gentle tug and the scientist came to his feet, clutching at his throat and choking. Of its own accord, the whip was slowly tightening, cutting off his air like a constrictor snake.

"I asked you a question," Trebuchet said with a harsh smile. "The jewel."

85

Leadbelly pawed ineffectually at the whip, his face turning red. "Gahhh –"

Trebuchet let him choke a moment more, and then whispered, "Release." The whip uncoiled and fell away. "Clever, *n'est-ce pas*? Another gift from Master Drache."

The scientist coughed loudly and attempted to maintain a little dignity. "The jewel, yes, of course." He waved at the mesas in the distance. "The pictographs all indicate an indigenous tribe of natives in this area, likely to have lived here for several hundred years."

"Not true," Coaler ventured. "No Indians. Not here. Never were."

"Then how do you explain the markers? Oh, they're here all right. They just don't want to be found."

"For the last time," Trebuchet snarled, *"where is the jewel?"*

"They have it, don't you see? The second set of glyphs points to the mesas. They must live there."

"For a smart man you seem to be an idiot far too often, Dr Leadbelly. There is no wildlife, no plants to speak of in this desolate place, nothing for a whole tribe to live on – why, we ourselves must bring in every kind of supply by wagon or rail." He snatched the map from the little man. "The mine was here for ten years before it was abandoned. Any Indians in the area would have raided it at least once or twice during that time."

"I tell you, these symbols do not lie!" Leadbelly's voice rose an octave. "The murals depict the jewel falling from the clouds, and the savages taking it for safe keeping." He stabbed a finger in the air. "In the mesa, somewhere."

Trebuchet studied the distant mountains for a long moment. "It would take for ever to search those rocks for another one of these caves. You'll have to do better than just some vague directions, my dear Doctor."

Leadbelly kicked at a loose stone. "I'm sure Master Drache will understand the situation when he returns. He is a scientist, as I am, and he comprehends the realities of projects like this, that it cannot all be done in an instant—"

His words were cut off by the crack-snap of Trebuchet's whip unfurling to its full length. The portly man hesitated, shocked rigid as the metal cord rose and fell like an impossibly long cobra; in the next instant, the whip had wrapped itself around his right arm and squeezed. He howled as blood welled up from under his sleeve.

"You have your orders. You will not wait for Drache," the Frenchman hissed. "You will find me the jewel, not a cave, not a map, but the jewel! Understand me, little troll?"

Leadbelly managed a pained nod.

Fivehawk had returned to the room the Hidden

People had granted him and not slept again. His thoughts were in turmoil still, even as the first rays of sunlight crept into the concealed valley. He watched the light sweep gently across the rows of plantings and the animal corrals, and was once more struck by the peculiar beauty of the place. He could understand why men like Grey Arrow would not wish to leave this perfect island of life, why they would rather go from birth to death here instead of seeing the outside world with all its flaws and horrors, from the tyrannies of weak men to the evils of monsters like Drache and his outriders.

And yet... Rivercloud, for all her ways and selfish motivations, also spoke the truth when she argued for the right to see beyond the borders of this little world. In their own ways, both were as right as they were wrong.

"What are you thinking, Wanderer?"

He smiled. "About you, Rivercloud."

She entered and sat beside him. "Good thoughts?" She was close, her breath warm on his face.

Fivehawk could sense her longing, her desire to leave the valley like a scent on the wind. "I wonder if you realize what you wish for," he said after a long moment. "Here, you are the daughter of a chief, feted and respected, courted by strong braves like Looks-Far. But out there —" he waved at the desert wilderness — "there you will be nothing more than just another Indian."

Rivercloud pulled a face. "I grow weary of this place. Of Father and of Looks-Far." She inched closer to him. "I could show you a way out, Fivehawk. A route through the tunnels even Grey Arrow could not find. We could escape and you could show me your world, as I have shown you mine."

He shook his head. "I gave my word. I will not leave until your father chooses my fate."

She turned away from him in disgust. "Men! Always talking of duty and honour and never of life."

Fivehawk looked into the sky. "You should cherish your time with your kith, Rivercloud. When they are gone, you will never have it again." Unbidden, a face rose in his mind; his sister smiling at him. For a split-second, it seemed as if it were she who sat beside him instead of Rivercloud. *Is she near?* he wondered. *In the mine or in another of Drache's foul camps?* Somehow, he knew she was still far, far away.

The girl saw the light in Fivehawk's eyes dim a little. "Your friend, the white man Tyler. He is on his way back to the prison of earth. I could help you escape, get to him."

"Tyler is not so foolish as to take on all of the outriders alone." Fivehawk sighed, but in his heart he knew that the reverse was true. "This is all wrong," he said suddenly. "We should be standing together to fight this evil, not divided and arguing among ourselves. We will turn around and find the world became ashes while we were quarrelling."

"The Faceless is just a story for children," Rivercloud said uncertainly.

"And so is The Heart of the World, so are the Hidden People, but does that make them any less real?"

She watched the rising sun for a moment. "My father will never help you, Wanderer. He will guard The Heart until he dies. As long as it is here, so will he be." Rivercloud paused. "Looks-Far will have you thrown into the pit. You must escape!"

Fivehawk shook his head. "Tyler would have been killed out of hand if I had not offered myself in his place. I cannot go back on that now."

"He is that good a friend? A white man?" She was incredulous.

"He is reckless, loud, foolish and barbaric ... but we are brothers in the mission against The Faceless. And yes, he is a friend."

Tyler's face wrinkled and he sneezed violently. "Trail dust," he said to himself. At a gallop, he had ridden back to the Burnt Hills mine, approaching from around the ridge to keep the outrider guards from noticing his advance. Now, as the dawn light strengthened and grew into morning, he was close to the perimeter fence.

He'd heard the heavy pop of detonation minutes earlier – Drache's men were obviously blasting early today – and he smiled. That might give him an opportunity. His only chance in busting out his uncle was to create confusion and get out in the mêlée. What Tyler needed was to get every prisoner and slave miner out and running all at once.

His horse gave a whinny and balked at the barbed wire, which hissed as it shifted over the sandy ground. Tyler felt in his saddlebags, recalling Tulsa's words the night before. Fire. They didn't like fire.

He drew out a bundle of cloth and opened it; inside were a dozen sticks of dynamite. Tyler grinned. They certainly were not going to like *this* kind of fire.

The first three sticks lit from a struck match and began popping and fizzing. Tyler tossed them over the fence towards the north, east and south, then lit one more and dropped it into the snarl of wire with a grimace. "Here's a hot meal for ya!"

The barbs grabbed at the dynamite, poking and probing it, sharp tips licking at it as a potential meal. But this was one snack that would give the wire the mother of all stomachaches.

The gunslinger had barely got into cover when the first explosives blew, almost as one. There were shouts and cries, then a fourth blast. Tyler urged his mount on and rode for the fence; the wire was blackened and shrunken, coiled in on itself, leaving a huge gap in the line. Tyler cracked his reins with a "Yah!" of encouragement to his mount and galloped in, a stink like burnt hair gusting past him.

Outriders and slaves alike were starting to spill out of their barracks as he dashed into the mine proper. Tyler threw another two sticks behind him, one dropping into the well and the other bouncing under a covered wagon. Luck was with him, and the dynamite in the well detonated a split-second before it hit the water, sending a column of droplets and stone chips ten feet into the air; the wagon was consumed in a blare of flame, blown into fragments of wood and canvas.

Tyler and his horse were a whirlwind, an unleashed force of nature as they charged into the camp. Guiding the beast with his knees, the gunslinger grabbed his Springfield rifle and drew a bead on one of the tower guards, who had his own rifle at the ready. He squeezed the trigger and was rewarded with a screech as the outrider fell to the dirt, clutching at his midriff.

As if the shot was a signal, the outriders began to open fire, shooting wildly at the rider and horse as they zigzagged between the buildings. A ragged cheer went up from the slaves as they realized that help might finally be at hand. As he passed one bunkhouse, Tyler reacted to avoid Ox's meaty paw as the fat man lashed out at him. Awakened by the blasts, still half-asleep and clad in his sweat-stained long johns, Ox made a clumsy play for Tyler and instead got a boot and spur in the face for his troubles. The outrider fell like a ton of bricks, and Tyler was already away, pulling his mount to a halt in the open ground between the prisoner huts.

"Come on!" he shouted at the top of his lungs. "Get out of here!"

Hesitation showed on many of the faces turned up at him. Tyler cursed and fired off a couple of shots into the air. "Run, you fools, run! This is a jailbreak!"

The crowd broke and stampeded towards the breach he'd made in the fence. Tyler caught a glimpse of another outrider, a heavy-set fellow with dark skin, shoving a wagon in the way to block them in. He grinned. That wouldn't be enough to stop them.

A voice broke through his concentration, just one single word hitting like a lightning bolt in his mind. "Gabriel?"

Tyler wheeled around; a dirty, dishevelled man stared at him, wide-eyed.

"Uncle Bill," he managed. The moment froze in time like a fly caught in amber as emotion flooded into Tyler's mind. After all this time, searching through the vacant ghost of his home in Stonetree, chasing down to the mine, and all the strange, terrible things he had witnessed in between, Tyler was reunited with the man who had raised him as his own. His reason for being here stood right in front of him, blinking in disbelief.

There were a million things he wanted to say to the old man, apologies for leaving all those years ago, for forgetting to write, for just forgetting; but instead he grabbed Bill's arm and pulled his uncle on to his horse.

"Hang on," he gritted. "I'll get you out of here, I promise. No matter what it takes."

Bill barely had time to cling on before Tyler snapped his reins and the horse bolted like a loosed bullet. They ran full tilt towards the broken fence, gunfire barking and lead singing through the air around them. Tyler's face split with a fearless grin. He hadn't needed Fivehawk's help after all, never mind him and his chicken-hearted pals hiding out in the caves – he was Gabriel Tyler, and he had done it alone! That robber baron Drache would be cursing his name when he heard about this!

They were almost upon the wagon; Coaler stood, legs spread on the flatbed of the buckboard, tugging at a canvas cloth that covered an angular object beneath it. Tyler took aim – one shot and the outrider would be out, permanently.

With a flourish, Coaler whipped the canvas over his shoulder and away. He laughed darkly. On the wagon sat a cluster of pipes, all pointed into the air like the tubes of a church organ. He pushed forward, and the array dropped to eye-level, the pipes swinging to point at the fleeing prisoners, spurts of gas hissing from extending rams and pistons.

"Holy Cats!" cried Bill.

The multiple mouths of a Gatling gun winked at them. Tyler had seen these massive weapons before, a circle of ten or more rifle barrels that rotated to fire a rapid salvo, but never one like this. Instead of a single circuit of tubes, three drums of them faced forward. Coaler laughed again and tugged on a lever.

The Gatling guns chattered into life with a sound like the mashing of metal teeth, and the ground at their feet erupted as the bullets chewed into the dust.

"Blocked!" shouted Bill.

Tyler swore under his breath, barely keeping control of his horse as the gunfire sent it into a mad panic. He pulled his mount around, catching sight of the main gates. *The gate! That's it! If I can get the gate open, I can still get them out!*

Doubling back, they raced through the prisoners who scattered under the withering fire from the guns, running a crooked course between huts and tents towards the mine camp's towering entrance. Ahead of them, Trebuchet stepped from the cover of the office shack and let his bullwhip unspool. He eyed the gunslinger and drew back his arm in a blur of motion.

Tyler's sights were elsewhere, aiming at the gatehouse, drawing a bead with his rifle. *Just one shot, gotta take out that gatekeeper!*

Uncle Bill had barely enough time for a wordless yell when the world suddenly spun around its axis and flipped upside down. Trebuchet roared triumphantly — his whip had caught the horse's foreleg exactly, entwining it and snaring the headlong animal. The dappled mare tumbled into a heap, catapulting Bill one way and Tyler the other. His rifle spun end-over-end through the air and hit the dirt like a thrown spear, the muzzle in the sand.

Tyler landed headfirst, rolling into a flip that miraculously brought him back to his feet. The young man was operating on pure instinct now, reacting without thinking. The weighty Colt Peacemaker six-gun was in his hand as he came up, searching for Trebuchet.

"Behind you!" cried a woman's voice. Tyler was startled; it was Tulsa, just a couple of yards away from him, her face a mask of fear. He whirled around, an instant too slow.

The stubby shotgun in Targa's hand barked, blasting a cloud of buckshot at his head. The rain of lead creased his face, raking bloody streaks across his skin and sending him spinning to the ground. A roaring blackness filled his vision and he sank into unconsciousness.

Targa sniffed archly and ejected the spent cartridges from her gun, studying Tulsa's ragged attire. "Take a good look at him, girlie," she sneered.

"That's what happens to men when they try to be heroes."

"He's still alive," Tulsa forced out, her eyes tearing.

Trebuchet stood over Tyler's form and nudged him with his boot. "We'll see."

7: DOUBLE CROSS

Tyler awoke piecemeal. Fragments of him regained consciousness one by one, gradually locking together to bring him back from the dark place where Targa's shotgun blast had sent him. Every joint in his body was aching, his head still ringing from the concussion of the gun's discharge.

He was inside one of the shabby buildings. Racks of glass bottles and benches were laid out in front of him, strewn with piles of paper and assorted junk. A few feet away, he spied a pile of gear — his hat, gunbelt, the contents of his saddlebags. He turned his head a little, flinching as pain shot through him. He was sitting in a barber's chair, wrists and ankles held in place by thick leather straps.

There was movement behind him, the sound of a person shifting, working at something. Tyler breathed slowly and gently tested the strength of the restraints. None of them budged. The gunslinger closed his eyes and cursed silently. He had been a fool, again! *Why do I never learn?* he chastised himself. *Why am I so pig-headed and stupid?* For one brief moment, he had been cocky enough to think that alone, he could rout the outriders and lead a jailbreak. All the way from the mesa valley, Tyler's anger at Fivehawk and the Hidden People had built until he had convinced himself that he didn't need them, he didn't care for their cowardly manners, that he could do the job on his own; but instead of doing it right, he rushed in — *yeah, a fool rushing in where angels fear to tread*, he thought bitterly — and royally messed the whole thing up.

He blinked. His face itched where the shotgun pellets had raked across his cheek, leaving fresh cuts and dried blood. An inch to the left, and Targa's shot would have turned his head into a red mist.

Damn Fivehawk! Damn him and his stupid legends! Tyler told himself, a sudden bright flare of ridiculous anger blazing through him, pointlessly blaming the Indian, while another voice in the back of his mind reminded him that Fivehawk had got him out of trouble once again. The Indian had put himself on the line, perhaps even sacrificed his own life to save Tyler's hide, but rather than admit to his own mistakes, the cowboy's runaway fury burnt like a brand. He shook his head to shake the thoughts away. He was just too angry to be realistic right now.

"He's awake," said Trebuchet's voice.

Leadbelly stepped in front of Tyler and studied him through his spectacles like an insect under a microscope. "Hmmph. Clearly an inferior specimen of the human male."

Tyler scowled. "You're no oil painting yourself, Tubby."

A snap of female laughter came from his left, and he smelt the mingled perfume of gunpowder and roses. "Mister Tyler, isn't it?" Targa stepped into his line of sight and pushed Leadbelly aside. The scientist frowned and moved to a nearby bench. She leant close to him. "Still alive. Well, well."

"Yeah," he managed, "your aim is lousy."

The smile on her face vanished and she slapped him, sending a fresh ring of pain through his skull.

"Let's not continue to waste time, shall we?" Trebuchet said. "Ask him."

Targa's smile returned; it was not a pretty sight. She held her hand up for him to see, four fingers and a thumb each with a pale-red nail at the tip. A muscle under her skin twitched and the nails grew in length, darkening, rising to a sharp point.

"I can gut you like a fish, carve off your skin like a surgeon," she husked.

Tyler gulped but said nothing. This was bad.

"The Indian. Where is he?"

"What Indian?" he lied automatically.

Targa sighed and slapped him again, this time

cutting his face a little more. The scratches sang with agony.

For the first time, Trebuchet passed in front of him, a thin plume of cigarette smoke wreathing his face. He gave Tyler an arch nod. "Fortune, she does not smile on you today, eh?"

"I'll live with it," Tyler said, with false bravado.

"Not for long," said the Frenchman. "We know the Indian is nearby..."

The words slipped out before he had a chance to think about them. "He's not coming here."

Targa paused and studied him. "How interesting. He's not lying. The little trail-rat means it."

Trebuchet made an amused noise. "A promising partnership broken so early on. How distressing." He took a step forward. "We no longer need you, then. Give me that revolver."

Leadbelly handed the Frenchman Tyler's handgun, and he spun the chamber, removing all but one bullet. With a flick of his wrist, he cocked the hammer and took aim between Tyler's eyes. "I've always wondered how many spins it would take to kill a man this way..."

He pulled the trigger and the hammer descended on an empty chamber with a hollow clap.

"That's one," said Targa.

Trebuchet spun the chamber and took aim again. Tyler's heart was pounding, hard enough it seemed to crack his ribs from the inside. He had to stall for time, but how? *Anything!* He thought to himself. *Just say anything!*

"I left the Indian behind," he said quickly. "He chickened out on me."

"Really?" said Trebuchet in a bored voice. He pulled the trigger. Another empty chamber. "That's two."

"He got himself a squaw, see, from some other tribe."

Leadbelly reached out and pushed the six-gun away from his head. "Another tribe? From around here, the mesas?"

"Yeah." Tyler blew out a breath, blinking sweat from his eyes.

Drache's minions exchanged glances. "It must be them," said Trebuchet.

"No other explanation," agreed Leadbelly.

Targa smiled and stepped forward with a length of bandage in her hand. "You know, Tyler, perhaps we might be able to come to some sort of agreement."

"Agreement?" he repeated, recoiling as the woman began delicately to clean and dress his wounds.

"That redskin left you twisting in the wind, eh? What kind of thing is that to do to a man, I ask you?" Trebuchet said in a reasonable tone. "I can't say I blame you, Tyler, for sneaking in here like you did. After all, you were only trying to do the right thing, eh? The right thing for the old man."

Tyler's blood ran cold. Uncle Bill. Did they know?

"If you've hurt him—" he began, but Targa shushed him like a mother admonishing a child.

"He's quite safe." She studied his face for a moment. "I think I see a family resemblance, don't you?"

"I'll tell you what," Trebuchet said, puffing on his cigarette, "I'll overlook this bit of rabble-rousing you did, and cut your old man loose, if you do me a favour in return, *n'est-ce pas?* A tiny thing, *très petite.*"

"That's the best offer you're going to get all day," Targa added.

"What do you want?" Tyler asked, the words like ashes in his mouth.

"This!" Leadbelly blurted, waving a piece of paper under his nose. "The mesa tribe have it." On the paper was a rough sketch of a faceted ball, a fist-sized jewel.

The glowing gemstone from the cavern. Tyler tried and failed to keep a glimmer of recognition from his face. Targa broke into a broad grin; she knew they had him.

Trebuchet nodded. "The old man for the jewel, then. An even trade. You take us to it, and you both walk free."

"What about the tribe? What about Fivehawk?"

Targa's smile twisted into a snarl. "What do you care about a bunch of filthy redskin savages? They obviously don't care a jot to let you get shot at by us!"

Trebuchet saw the hesitation and conflict in Tyler's eyes, and put an arm on the barber chair and spun it in a half-circle, turning him to face the other side of the hut. "Of course," he hissed in Tyler's ear, "we'll find them by ourselves sooner or later, it's just that sooner would be better."

Tyler's mouth went dry. He was staring at a crude operating table, on top of which an Indian man around the same age as Uncle Bill was lying. The man had sightless eyes and obscene vents cut into his throat.

"If you don't want to help us, the good Dr Leadbelly here can always use more subjects for his experiments."

Tyler looked at the floor. "You just want the gemstone? Nothing else?"

"Nothing else," repeated Targa.

"No killing? You just take the jewel and go, right?"

"Of course," Trebuchet said carefully. "If you help us find it, there will be no need for unnecessary bloodshed. I give you my word."

Tyler felt like a black chasm was opening up around him, swallowing him whole. He heard his own voice say "All right", and deep inside him, a part of his soul shrivelled up and died.

*　　*　　*

Trebuchet dismissed Leadbelly, directing him to prepare the other outriders for a raid, and had Coaler take Tyler outside. Targa toyed with a stiletto blade and eyed him.

"This has all the makings of a mistake."

"Oh, you worry too much, *cherie*. Fortune has dealt us an extra ace. This fool Tyler will lead us to the tribe, and we'll have this jewel before the day is out!"

"And then?"

The Frenchman smiled. "Then we'll kill him! And the old man too, just to be sure."

"These Indians ... they won't just let you waltz in and take the stone."

"They'll have no choice. With Master Drache's new aerial toy at our disposal, the outriders will be there before they know it." He stubbed out his cigarette. "And once I possess the jewel, I'll wipe them off the face of the earth."

"And what about Drache? He'll be here tomorrow."

"And I'll be ready for him!" He picked up Leadbelly's notebook and held it out to her. "The doctor is quite talkative about his discoveries, you know. I learnt much from my little morning sojourn with him."

She flipped through the pages, skipping over complex sketches and blocks of spidery text. "Such as?"

"The true value of the jewel. You were right when you said that power is Drache's only true love. According to the little troll, the gemstone is some kind of cousin to that foul sky rock, 'an energetic material', I think he called it, but the effects are much different."

"You mean like reversed? Not poisonous to us?"

"Nothing so crude. It's like a streak of lightning captured in a bottle, a key made out of light."

"Now you sound like that fat egghead." Targa shut the notebook with a snap. "Babbling scientific nonsense. A key? A key to what?"

Trebuchet stabbed a finger at Leadbelly's map of the mine, pointing at the location of the metallic chamber they had encountered at the lowest level. "A key to this. A key to the power within!" He nodded to himself. "If we wait for Drache's return, whatever the chamber holds will become his and we will gain nothing. But if we take the initiative, if we dare to proceed…"

Targa's eyes lit up with greed. "We can open it before he does. Take the riches inside for ourselves."

"Ah yes, *cherie*," Trebuchet breathed. "Then we will be the Masters."

Tyler stood slump-shouldered in front of the contraption Leadbelly was working on, his face set and grim. His mind churned conflicted thoughts like a whirlpool, until he thought he might scream out loud. *How have I come to this?* he asked himself. *I'm an ally of the scum of the earth.*

"You'll never be able to get into the valley, even if I show you where the entrance is," he said morosely.

Leadbelly barked out a laugh. "Don't worry. We're not going to waste time going through the front door. We're going to fall from the sky like thunder!"

Other members of Drache's outrider band had gathered nearby, the huge Ox toying with his pig-ring while Rattler and Coaler loaded their guns. Leadbelly fixed Tyler with a cock-eyed glare and waved at the device in front of him. "Prepare to be amazed!" he shrilled theatrically and stepped forward to tug on a bright-red lever. The thing was like a metal pillbox, roughly the size of a stagecoach but raised off the ground by four arched legs ending in skids instead of wide wheels. Curiously, a number of tethers led from its flanks to hooks hammered into the ground. From its roof, a vast and shapeless canvas bag drooped, lying across it like a giant discarded bed-sheet. Leadbelly struggled with the lever for a moment and grunted as it shifted; in reply, the box shuddered and emitted gusts of steam.

"Arise!" chuckled the portly scientist. "Arise, my pretty!"

The canvas shifted and moved, unfolding itself like a tent being erected by invisible hands. Tyler's jaw dropped open as the cloth began to take on a recognizable shape, stubby and cylindrical.

"It's a balloon!" he gasped. Tyler recalled stories he'd heard about gas-bag airships and inventors who spoke of them as one day making the railroads obsolete, pictures he'd seen in books and the like – but he'd never seen the real thing.

Coaler pushed him towards the metal gondola. "Get in."

As they boarded, Ox busied himself untying the guide ropes while Leadbelly sat in the single chair at the bow, working a series of levers and handles. With a sibilant hiss, the blimp's inflation ceased and a pair of short wings extended from the flanks of the gondola.

Despite the grimness of the situation, Tyler could not resist the urge to peer out of one of the pillbox slots to watch the ground fall away as they rose into the air.

"Get him strung up," said Rattler.

Ox grabbed Tyler's shoulders and the gunslinger tensed, expecting them to open the hatch and throw him to his death, but instead the big man strapped a harness to him and connected it to a cable dangling from the ceiling. He glanced around – each of the outriders had done the same.

Leadbelly adjusted the wings and let the wind catch them, sending the tiny airship streaking forward like a galleon under full sail.

The rough desert landscape flashed past underneath them, hundreds of feet below, suddenly giving way to the rocks of the mesa and then an island of greenery. Tyler looked away, a sickening giddy sensation in his gut, and into the eyes of the other outriders. They all studied him like a predator watches a cornered prey.

Fivehawk stooped to take a cupful of water from the well and drank deeply, glancing around him at the rows of plantings and the playing children. He frowned when he noticed Looks-Far watching him intently, the brave's hand on the butt of his pistol. The Indian turned away, tipping his head back to drain the cup.

Something passed in front of the sun, not a bird or a cloud, but an odd rounded shape. He held up a hand to shield his eyes. Looks-Far followed suit, both men searching the sky for the strange object.

Then, without warning, smoke and fire began to rain from the air.

Tyler swore at Coaler and dived across the tiny cabin at him. Ox easily intercepted him and forced him back to the floor.

"No killing!" Tyler shouted. "Trebuchet said no killing!"

"The Frenchman says a lot of things," hissed Rattler.

Coaler ignored the argument and continued his task, dropping glass bottles of nitro-glycerine and smoke bombs through a porthole in the gondola.

Tyler felt his gorge rise as puffs of flame erupted amid the green of the valley, trees suddenly blowing apart into splinters and fields turning instantly into infernos. Cries of alarm and screams reached up to them from the people below.

"Where's the jewel?" Leadbelly grated. "The quicker we get it, the quicker we'll leave these poor wretches alone."

Tyler pointed towards Grey Arrow's chambers. "There," he spat.

Rattler nodded and in unison the outriders lifted their neckerchiefs to cover their noses and mouths. Ox prodded Tyler and he sluggishly did the same.

Leadbelly guided the airship as low as he could, just above the tree line, and turned it to hover close to the chamber entrance. He threw a lever and something unlocked beneath Tyler's feet; in the next second the floor of the gondola opened along its length and the outriders dropped to the ground, the harnesses singing as they played out the cables.

He landed in a heap, the wind rushing out of his lungs in a loud cough. Ox grabbed him by the shoulder and pulled him to his feet, like a child picking up a rag doll. Tyler glanced up; Leadbelly was visible, still nursing the wings and rudders to hold the airship steady amid the updraughts from the newly created fires. His mind was in turmoil – there had to be some way he could stop this, turn things back before they went too far...

Coaler gestured with his gun. "Show us."

Tyler nodded sullenly and unhooked himself. "This way."

Fivehawk crashed through the smouldering brush, half-blinded by the smoke and ash. All around he could hear shouts and cries from the tribesmen as they raced to put out the fires; he nodded to himself in understanding. Of course, in such a small valley as this, a fire could wipe out everything in hours, so the Hidden People would react quickly to douse the flames as soon as they could – but in the confusion, the cause might be missed. The thing in the sky must have started the fires, he reasoned, as a diversion to draw attention away.

Away from the only item of value in the valley.

Fivehawk quickened his pace, able only to see a hand's-length in front of his face – and crashed headlong into another rushing form.

The two figures went down in a tangle of limbs, falling over each other. Fivehawk rolled to his feet, expecting to face off against an outrider; Looks-Far stared back at him, his eyes wild with panic and fury.

"The Heart o' the World!" the brave shouted. Clearly, he too understood the reason for the surprise attack.

Fivehawk nodded and helped him to his feet. "We must hurry!"

Coaler kicked open the wooden door to the inner chamber with a savage blow and disappeared inside. Ox shoved Tyler in after him and followed, while Rattler came after him. The outriders wasted no time when they entered the room, ignoring the beauty and splendour of the murals on the walls; they were numb to it, brutal and unfeeling.

"The stone," Coaler said, his face splitting in a grin. "Get it." He took a step forward and something blurred in front of him, shrieking like a banshee.

Tyler recoiled as a knot of rock near the far wall suddenly shimmered into the shape of a woman and leapt at Coaler's throat; Rivercloud.

Ox raised his gun and let off a shot, but Tyler sank an elbow into his ribs, knocking the big outrider's aim wide.

Rivercloud sank her nails into Coaler's neck, but the dark man struck her hard across the head and she fell to the floor, dazed.

"Well, looky here." Rattler grinned. "A feisty one. Let's take her with us."

Coaler enveloped The Heart with his huge hand and dropped it into a sack, the blue glow fading from the paintings and ornaments on the walls. "We go."

Fivehawk and Looks-Far emerged close to Grey

Arrow's chambers. The silent shape of the airship startled both men as it drifted in the smoky air.

"What is it?" Looks-Far asked, his face a mixture of shock and amazement. "Is this some kind of white man's magic? A cloud made of iron and cloth?"

"A machine." Fivehawk nodded. "It is a flying machine, one of Drache's mechanical creations."

"But it flies!" The brave gaped. "Like a honeybee on the wind!"

"More like a hornet," Fivehawk grated. "This iron beast will have a sting."

The outriders boiled out of the chamber doors and raced for the dangling cables beneath the airship. Fivehawk's breath caught in his throat as he saw Rivercloud struggling in Rattler's grip. There were three more, two he recognized from the camp and another he found oddly familiar.

Neither Indian spoke; as one they leapt from their cover, whooping war cries and dived on the invaders, catching them by surprise as they fastened their harnesses. Fivehawk crashed into Rattler and the outrider released Rivercloud, swinging at the Indian.

"Run, Rivercloud, run!" he shouted, and she obeyed. Fivehawk was ready for Rattler, slashing with his buck knife. The outrider sidestepped and slapped at the harness on his chest. Fivehawk lunged, but with a snap of cogwheels, Rattler shot up into the air, reeled in by the airship.

Coaler struggled with Looks-Far, the brave pressing a tomahawk into his face while the dark outrider pushed back with a lengthy hunting blade. Coaler butted at the Indian with his head and knocked the small axe to the grass, pressing the attack; Looks-Far caught the bigger man's hand on pure reflex and twisted it back at him.

Coaler grunted and coughed out a mouthful of olive-coloured blood as his own blade sank into his heart. "I'm ... dead," he wheezed.

Looks-Far clutched at the bag in the outrider's death-grip, but felt the world suddenly turn about him. Ox bodily picked up the brave and tossed him back into the trees.

Fivehawk swung at the other outrider and missed him, but passed close enough to pull the bandanna from his face. The Indian's eyes widened. "Tyler?" he breathed, the gunslinger's troubled features looking back at him in dismay, suddenly revealed. "What—?"

His words were cut off by Ox, who grabbed a handful of his jacket and dragged him backwards, twisting him over and up. Fivehawk's vision spun as he flew a good three yards through the air to land face down in the sand.

Ox forced Tyler back into the airship with a heavy shove, the gondola ringing with impacts as they rose.

"Those blasted savages are shooting at us!"

Leadbelly snarled, glancing over his shoulder. "Are you all in? Did you get it?"

"Got it," Rattler said, holding the sack, "but Coaler's gone."

"Toss him out, then. We don't need any extra ballast."

Rattler flicked at Coaler's harness and the corpse fell away, tumbling into the trees like a broken puppet.

Tyler felt as if a claw had reached into his gut and torn out his innards, made him hollow and empty. *What have I done?* he asked himself, and answered with shattering certainty; *I've betrayed the trust of a friend.* He stared hard at the sack in Rattler's hands, his thoughts racing.

Fivehawk struggled to his feet as the airship gusted away on the wind, clutching at his bruised ribs. It seemed as if his entire world had come crashing down around him; the things he took for granted, for certain, shattered in an instant and turned inside out. Tyler's face beneath the bandanna, the haunted look in the cowboy's eyes, all were etched into his mind like chisel-marks on stone. The Indian felt the pit of his stomach fill with ice; had he been so bold to think that he could have beaten The Faceless, if its influence could turn Tyler to its cause and cut out the very core of the Hidden People's world in mere moments?

Grey Arrow stumbled towards him, the Elder's face ashen. "We are lost!" he cried, tears filling his eyes. "The Heart is gone! Everything that we are has been taken from us! We are lost!"

Fivehawk nodded slowly. *Lost indeed*, he mused.

8: THE RECKONING

For the longest time, no one spoke; the Hidden People gathered mournfully around Grey Arrow, the air still heavy with lingering smoke.

The Elder stood on the threshold to his chambers, unable to enter. "Our purpose has been taken from us," he breathed. "The Heart of the World has been stolen."

A mutter of disbelief ran through the natives. A few voices cursed and rose in anger. Fivehawk said nothing, offering Looks-Far a hand to pick himself up from the ground. The brave took it gladly; it seemed that during the fury of the outrider attack, Looks-Far's distrust of him had fled.

The crowd parted to allow Rivercloud to approach her father. Grey Arrow hugged her and brushed her unkempt hair from her eyes. "My child," he said quietly, "I was afraid they might have killed you."

"I would have perished if the Wanderer had not rescued me." Rivercloud would not meet his gaze. "Father, I failed you. I failed our tribe and the Great Spirit. I did not stop the intruders."

"You could not have," Looks-Far offered. "Fivehawk and I could not way-lay them, and we were two to your one. Their flying machine set the fires to divide us and scatter our strength."

Rivercloud said nothing; she seemed unconvinced.

Voices broke out from the crowd as the reality of the crime set in, some in fear that the Great Spirit would be angry at them for their failure, others crying out for revenge, retaliation. Grey Arrow released his daughter and held up a hand for quiet.

"My people. We cannot let this tragedy shatter our lives. We must seek guidance from the Great Spirit."

He turned to face Fivehawk, his gaze steady. "Fivehawk, son of Elk's Brother. I am indebted to you for saving the life of my only child, and for that I release you from your obligation to me. I see now you are no threat to our people." The Elder gestured at him, addressing his tribe. "This Wanderer came to us with tales about a demon. He came with a warning about The Faceless and we did not hear him!"

A ripple of emotion fanned out through the crowd; terror. Children hid behind mothers' skirts while men gripped weapons in grim fear.

Looks-Far placed a hand on Fivehawk's shoulder. "Forgive me, Wanderer. I was wrong to doubt you. When these invaders attacked, you fought to protect our land as if it were your own."

Fivehawk gave a small nod. His thoughts were elsewhere, in chaos. Tyler, the gunslinger he had ridden with since his first encounter with Drache and the minions of The Faceless, had been there with the outriders. Fivehawk was unable to bring voice to the idea that Gabriel Tyler had switched sides, put aside the honesty in his heart and joined Drache's men. It could not be so...

Grey Arrow was speaking. "The failure here is not my daughter's – it is mine. For too long, I have clung to the conceit that our secret valley is apart from the world beyond the mesa. We forbid our people to venture past our territories, but we cannot stop the outside from coming here." He hesitated; the clearing was silent. "Fivehawk brought a warning and a plea for help, but I chose not to hear him because I feared what his words might mean. I was blind and deaf, and now see what I have brought to my people."

"Father," Rivercloud broke in, "you were only doing what you thought was right for us. For me."

The old man shook his head. "That is no excuse. I have brought shame to us."

"No!" Looks-Far shouted suddenly. "We cannot let this victory go to The Faceless, for it can only be the demon who would seek to steal The Heart of the World – we must answer Fivehawk's call to arms and take back what is ours!" He turned to face the Indian. "You asked for braves to liberate the slaves in the prison of earth, did you not? We will give them to you!"

Grey Arrow studied the faces of his people. "Such a battle would be costly. Lives will be lost. It could mean the end of our tribe."

"And if we stay and do nothing?" said Looks-Far. "It will also be the end, but a slow and painful one, a death by venom and sloth instead of in battle."

Grey Arrow nodded to Fivehawk. "Wanderer, you know more of this enemy than any of us. If we fight, do we have a chance?"

"I cannot answer that," Fivehawk said quietly, "but I trust in the Great Spirit."

"Then it shall be war, son of Elk's Brother. You shall lead our party into the enemy's stronghold." The Elder's voice rose and took on new strength. "Hear me, my people. Gather the braves and their weapons for battle, and we will bring a whirlwind to the servants of The Faceless that will wipe them from our lands!"

Rivercloud's voice carried through the air, even as the crowd cheered the chief's words. "My Father, what if we cannot recover The Heart of the World? What then?"

Grey Arrow's face hardened into a warrior's aspect. "Then, child, we will deny it to them. I swear by the Sacred Hoop, I will shatter it with my own bare hands before I allow the demon to possess it!"

The tribe scattered in all directions, making

preparations for combat. Fivehawk sank to his haunches and sat on a fallen log, his eyes fixed on a distant nowhere. He blinked with a start when Rivercloud delicately kissed him on the cheek.

"Thank you for my life, Wanderer," she breathed.

He gave a shaky nod. "You would have done no less for me."

She studied him for a moment. "You are troubled, Fivehawk, and not by the fear of battle. What is wrong?"

"I cannot –" he began, words failing him. "I think I may have lost a friend today."

"The white man?" she asked. "You think he may be dead?"

"Or worse." He could barely bring himself to form the words in his mind. *Tyler may be my enemy now.* He forced a smile and met her gaze. "Rivercloud, I wonder if you know how much Looks-Far cares about you," he said, changing the subject.

She shrugged. "Perhaps. But he is too protective of me. I'm not a child!"

"I saw the emotion in his eyes when the outriders captured you. He would have fought every single one of them to save your life."

Rivercloud said nothing, mulling over his words. Looks-Far emerged from the brush with two other braves, bearing a body between them.

"Fivehawk, look! The dark-skinned outrider fell from the flying machine."

He examined the corpse; Coaler's body was twisted at an unnatural angle, his limbs broken in dozens of places from the fall.

"We took his weapons," one of the braves said. "We'll turn them on his masters!"

Fivehawk nodded absently and drew Looks-Far's blade from the corpse's chest. "Look here," he said gravely, showing the greenish ichor that filled the wound. "This is how we know the minions of The Faceless and the servants of the man they call Drache. The influence of evil upon them pollutes their blood as it does the world, staining it."

Looks-Far took back his knife and examined it. "If they bleed," he growled, "then we can kill them."

Taking a deep breath of fresh air, Tyler stepped from the airship gondola and shrugged off the coat and hat he'd taken from the unfortunate Doglin. Suddenly, wearing the clothes of an outrider made him feel soiled and dirty somehow. Targa and Trebuchet were waiting and he gave them both a defiant look. *If I'm gonna take a bullet, I'll do it as myself*, he reasoned.

Targa eyed him, her hands cradling her short-barrelled shotgun as if it were a baby, a hungry expression on her face.

Leadbelly left Rattler inside the airship, securing the gas pump for the envelope, and pushed past Tyler with a sack in his hands, holding it up.

"Success!" he shrilled. "I have secured the jewel!" Ox followed suit, chuckling aloud.

Trebuchet gave Tyler a mocking bow. "Thank you for your help, Mister Tyler. You held up your end of the bargain, as I knew you would." He snapped his fingers. "Fetch the old man."

Targa let the shotgun drop to a ready position. "Time for us to keep our promise, right?"

Ever since he'd awoken in the barber's chair with Targa's claws about his face, Tyler had been nursing a small, faint fantasy that he might actually still be able to escape with Uncle Bill alive; now that tiny flame of hope guttered out and died under the cold wind of reality. Targa was going to put right the mistake she'd made when he attacked the camp and blow his head clean off with that nasty little cannon of hers. *Why does every dumb choice I make always end with me staring death in the face?* he asked himself.

Trebuchet snatched the sack from Leadbelly and drew out the massive gemstone. Tyler could have sworn he saw a trickle of drool on Targa's chin as the sunlight glinted and flashed off the huge jewel.

"Can you feel that?" Trebuchet breathed, the blue glow of the orb flickering around his fingers where he held it. "It's *alive*."

Leadbelly rubbed his face nervously. "I, uh, have some concerns," he began, drawing a pointed glare from Targa, "Master Drache was most insistent that I contact him the moment we located the—"

Trebuchet shook his head. "No! We cannot wait for him to return ... we must exploit this opportunity now!"

Targa underscored the Frenchman's point by prodding Leadbelly with the shotgun. "Understand, little troll?"

"Yes, of course. It's just that the effects of the jewel are—"

Targa prodded him into silence as Tulsa approached, supporting Bill Tyler with one arm. Gabriel's uncle had twisted his leg as he fell from his horse, and could only manage a slow, shuffling walk.

"Ah," smiled Targa. "The family's all here."

Tulsa shot her a venomous look and guided Bill to his nephew's side. The woman helped Tyler to hold him up. "Good luck," she whispered, thrusting something into his hand, unseen by the outriders. Tyler hid his surprise and palmed the object, running his fingers over it; it was a derringer pistol, a tiny two-shot holdout gun.

"Now step away," Targa barked, and Tulsa did as she was ordered.

"I'm sorry, Uncle Bill," Tyler husked. "I guess I'm not as quick as I thought I was."

The old man managed a smile. "Sure you are, son. I'm just sorry things turned out this way."

"I suppose we should let you go, hmm?" Trebuchet said idly. "That is what we agreed, isn't it?"

Tyler felt an odd kind of calm come over him.

"Tell me, in all your life has there ever been a time when you didn't lie to someone?"

A nerve jumped in Trebuchet's face and his false good humour vanished. "What do you know, trail-rat? You're a sentimental fool and your time has just about run out. In an hour I'll be the most powerful man in the world and you'll be taking a dirt nap."

Tyler turned himself so he could see the airship from the corner of his eye and cocked the derringer's hammer with his thumb. "Get ready to hit the deck." he whispered to his uncle.

Targa made a show of taking aim. "Two barrels on my gun," she smiled, "and two targets to shoot at. How convenient!"

In spite of himself, Tyler grinned. Targa saw his expression and hesitated, her finger tightening on the trigger. Tyler pointed the derringer into the airship, recalling the rotten-egg stink that had filled the interior of the airship, remembering the chemistry lessons he'd learnt as a boy. The stubby little blimp floated because its canvas envelope was pumped full of hydrogen – and hydrogen had a real problem with sparks. The gunslinger pulled the tiny pistol's trigger and shoved his uncle towards the ground. The twin twenty-two calibre bullets shot through the hatch and hit the gas pump squarely on the hose where Rattler was securing it. The outrider had time to see the flash of hot lead skipping off iron before the airship exploded into a fireball.

The hydrogen-filled cigar burst like an overripe fruit, sending a cascade of orange flame through the air, scattering streaks of fire, fragments of canvas, metal and Rattler to the four points of the compass. A dozen blazes started at once as hot shrapnel collided with dry wood or ignited barrels of blasting powder.

Everyone on their feet when the airship blew had been flung back ten feet and tossed to the ground. Leadbelly rolled to his knees and screamed. "My precious aircraft! Destroyed!"

Targa got to her feet and swore. A wall of fire had cut her off from Tyler and his uncle. She swore savagely and kicked at the fat scientist. "You dolt! You never said anything about that contraption being explosive!"

Trebuchet ignored them both, fighting down a moment of panic until he found the jewel where it had fallen from his hands. Ox carefully dusted the sand from it and gingerly handed it back to him. "Shut up, both of you," he ordered. "We have work to do."

"Work?" Targa was incredulous. "The camp is on fire!"

The Frenchman smiled faintly, lost in the play of light inside the jewel. "Never mind. We don't need it any more." He helped Leadbelly to his feet. "Come, Doctor. Lead on."

"Wh-where?" the fat man stuttered.

Trebuchet pointed towards the gaping dark void of the mine entrance. "Why, to the chamber of course.

We have an experiment to perform."

Ox hesitated, the big man's porcine face screwed up in an almost comical, baby-like expression of confusion. Targa poked him in the ribs.

"Something wrong, piggy?"

He nodded slowly. "Master Drache said that…"

"Drache's not here!" Targa barked, and Ox flinched. "You do what I say, understand me?"

"Yes, ma'am," the outrider replied thickly. "What you say."

"Then get in there!" Targa grunted, slapping him with a gloved hand towards the mouth of the mine.

The Indians halted as one as the fountain of fire erupted into the sky. Spread out across the ridge, Fivehawk and Looks-Far led twenty braves from the Hidden People, and – much to the horror of her father and husband-to-be – Rivercloud. They exchanged anxious glances as they watched the flames lick out to engulf parts of the slave camp stockade. Overhead, a solitary crow circled, perhaps attracted by the chance of stealing a little carrion meat from the helpless slaves.

"What was that?" asked Rivercloud.

Fivehawk nodded grimly. "A sign."

Looks-Far drew his gun and whooped. "We ride!" he cried, and the braves spurred their mounts on, down towards the camp.

*   *   *

Tyler and Uncle Bill stumbled away from the blazing wreck of the airship, picking their way past the dozens of small fires that had started in the wake of the explosion. The old man wheezed and coughed, straining. For a worrying moment, the two of them almost collapsed in a heap until a third set of hands appeared to support them – Tulsa.

"Smart move with that holdout gun, miss." Tyler smiled. "Thanks."

Tulsa frowned. "I kinda thought you'd shoot those outriders with it, not start an inferno!"

Tyler shrugged. "Hey, I improvised."

"Yes, thank you, Muriel. You're a smart one," added Bill.

"Muriel?" said Tyler. "Your name is Muriel?"

Tulsa scowled. "My real name. But nobody calls me that."

"Well, Muriel from Tulsa, thanks anyhow. I guess I made a pretty poor outrider, huh?"

"I could see it in your eyes." She smiled. "You got a good streak in there. Of course, it's still hidden under all that bravado and cocky swaggering."

They settled Bill Tyler down on to a buckboard. Gunfire echoed around the mine amid the chaos of the conflagration. "We gotta get out of this place," Gabriel said. "Leave this all behind and make a break for it."

Despite his fatigue, Bill's voice took on an angry tone. "Didn't I teach you anything, lad? You can't be thinking of yourself all the time!"

Tyler grimaced; the old man's words, his tone of voice were exactly the same as they'd been when he was a boy, and they brought back memories of spankings and punishments for childhood misdeeds. "I came here to save you!"

"But what did you do to get here, huh? You stole that rock for those filthy jaspers, didn't you? Took another man's property to protect my old hide." Bill shook his head. "I taught you better than that, Gabriel. I'd rather have gone blind in that hell-hole than have you steal to save me."

Tyler stood up, anger boiling to the surface, about to explode into fury – and hesitated. *Damn the old man if he wasn't right*. Tyler kicked hard at a stone. "I didn't have a choice, Uncle Bill. They would have killed you, and I couldn't let that happen, no matter what."

The old man sighed. "I know, son. I know you were trying to do the right thing."

"I was going to give it back," Tyler said lamely, his words ringing hollow even to his own ears. "I figured I'd get you free and then get the stone back for those Indians..."

"There's still time," said Tulsa. "I heard Trebuchet talking with the woman, Targa. Something about the mine, on the lowest level."

Tyler glanced back towards the mine entrance and weighed his options. In the end, he really had no choice. "You take this old coot and get him to safety," he told Tulsa, "I gotta go and put something right."

Tulsa wavered for a second, then planted a quick kiss on his cheek. "For luck," she explained, "but if you tell anyone I did that, I'll bust your face."

Tyler laid a hand on his uncle's chest. "I'll be back before you know it."

The outriders were totally unprepared for the Hidden People's attack. Parts from the airship had burnt gaps in the wire fence, making the barbs curl up and cower, allowing the Indians to stream through at full gallop. Looks-Far split off with a handful of braves and shot a salvo of arrows into the gate guards. The outriders crashed to the ground from their towers, pin-cushioned by the shafts. In moments, the gates were open, and the slaves looked on in disbelief.

Fivehawk stood high in his saddle and filled his lungs with air. "Freedom!" he shouted. "You are all free! Take the wounded and leave this place!"

A surge of strength seemed to well up in the weather-beaten, tired faces of the workers as they understood that suddenly, unexpectedly, liberation was at hand. Some broke for the gate, throwing their loads of stone and rock to the ground, while others took up weapons from their fallen overseers and joined in the fight. The Burnt Hills mine was in the throes of a revolution, and the oppressors were outnumbered three-to-one.

Rivercloud's cry jerked Fivehawk's head around. "There!" She pointed.

Fivehawk squinted through the smoke to see Tyler racing towards the mouth of the mine, his back to them and a purposeful aspect to his gait. In a flash, the Indian had brought his rifle to bear, sighting the running cowboy dead centre. He cocked the weapon; a single shot would bring Tyler to the ground.

His hand tensed on the trigger but did not move; with his own eyes, Fivehawk had seen Tyler in the raiding party that had stolen The Heart of the World. He knew with icy certainty that Drache's outriders would never have discovered the location of the secret valley without help. Tyler had to be guilty. He *had* to be.

And yet he could not pull the trigger. The words of the old shaman Sleeping Fox echoed through his mind – *the Spirit Road must be shared* – and he knew that the prophecy called for him to fight The Faceless side-by-side with Tyler.

Rivercloud was shocked. "You're going to kill your friend!"

The moment seemed to stretch into hours before the rifle fell from Fivehawk's hands. He watched Tyler disappear into the mine, never knowing how close he had come to death.

Fivehawk sighed. "Tyler was with the outriders when they stole The Heart," he said carefully. "He must have helped them."

She shook her head. "It cannot be. You would never risk your life for a man who would do such a thing. A Wanderer would not be so foolish."

"There's only one way to find out. I'm going after him."

"I will come as well," said Rivercloud defiantly. Fivehawk moved to stop her, but she brushed him away. "We have no time to argue, Wanderer!"

The Indian said nothing and rode on, towards the mine entrance. His hand strayed to the medicine bundle around his neck and a sudden flash of uncertainty shot through his mind; Gabriel Tyler's life had been in his hands and Fivehawk had let him live. But had he made the right choice?

9: DARK HEART

Trebuchet led Targa and the outriders into the depths of the mine with a spring in his step. Leadbelly eyed the tall Frenchman.

"We have no way to know what we will find in the chamber," he ventured. "I fear that opening it without Master Drache's guidance will be a mistake."

"So noted," said Trebuchet. "Shall we continue?"

They stepped into the lift and Ox tugged the bell-rope. As the platform descended, Targa shot Trebuchet a concerned look. "What if the twerp is right?"

Trebuchet barked out a laugh. "What's this?" He grinned. "The fearless Targa afraid of the unknown?" He looked around the confines of the elevator, at the apprehension visible on Ox, Targa and Leadbelly's faces. "We have nothing to be afraid of, so long as I have this!" He produced the jewel from the cloth sack held in his hand. The actinic blue light from within the massive gemstone wavered and slowly began to pulse, like a beating heart.

Leadbelly's jaw dropped open in shock. "Oh my."

"You see?" Trebuchet yelled, delighted. "It knows we are close!"

"It's just a rock," Targa growled. "It doesn't know anything."

The Frenchman shook his head and grabbed her hand. "You're wrong." He pulled her towards the stone. "Touch it. Touch your destiny!"

Targa struggled. "I don't want to! Let me go!"

He scowled and released her. "You foolish, spiteful woman. You like to play at being dangerous, but the truth is that you're a scared little child. Run back to Drache then, girl, if you're too afraid to usurp him." Trebuchet stroked the jewel. "Inside that chamber are riches and powers the like of which we've never seen – all we have to do is take them!"

Targa licked her lips but said nothing. Trebuchet smiled. Her greed had won out over her fears.

Leadbelly chewed his lip and looked away. Ever since they had strode arrogantly into his laboratory, the scientist had known Trebuchet and Targa were lying, plotting, concealing an agenda of their own – and now here it was, out in the open. They planned to seize the contents of the chamber and double-cross Master Drache ... and yet Leadbelly was surprised at how little that bothered him. True, he had often demonstrated loyalty to Drache and been rewarded, but the lure of the chamber's secrets set his mouth watering. The possibilities, the

134

undiscovered mysteries lurking inside smothered the twinge of fear he felt at the thought of his master's wrath. Without even knowing it, Leadbelly realized that he had already betrayed Drache to come this far, seduced by the need to know what existed beyond the metal walls of the chamber. *So be it*, he thought, *and if these self-important dolts destroy themselves along the way, then so much the better!*

The scientist fished in one of his cavernous pockets as the elevator fell past a final level marker. "We should take some of the formula now, to hold off the effects of the sky rock."

"No need." Trebuchet smiled. "The jewel is protection enough."

The scientist was about to protest, but realized that he felt none of the ill effects the jade-like stone caused. He blinked at the jewel. "It must be protecting us, blocking the poison. Incredible!"

At the lowest level of the mine they exited the lift. Ox rounded up the few slave workers still chipping at the stone walls and herded them into the elevator.

"Send them away," said Trebuchet. "We don't need any witnesses."

Targa picked her way warily through the mine works, as nervous as a cat. "You have no idea of what is waiting for us in there, do you?" she grated, pointed at the uncovered section of smooth metal wall.

Trebuchet tossed the jewel in the air and caught it with his other hand. The throbbing play of colour and light was getting quicker now, sending strobes of blue around the cavern. "Drache wants what is in there," he began. "That's reason enough for me to want to take it from him."

Ox and Leadbelly shifted uncomfortably, and the Frenchman cocked his head. "What's wrong, *mes amis*? Surely I'm not witnessing an attack of loyalty for Master Drache?" He laughed again. "What would you rather have, I ask you? Orders from a man who leaves you here in this wilderness to rot, or my undying gratitude and sharing nature? Ha-ha!"

Even as Leadbelly sweated and worried, the analytical part of his nature was studying the chamber, taking advantage of the protective power of the jewel. The blue light played about the walls, illuminating dim lines of symbols and design. He recognized them at once as wards, fragments of holy text that tribal shamans often used as markers and warnings of evil spirits; it was hoped that the strength of the sacred words would hold back the demons. Each one of the wards promised death and ruination to any that would venture past them. The symbols were the same as those he'd glimpsed in the marker chambers on the surface, only much, much older – perhaps even in the order of thousands of years.

Trebuchet approached the metal wall; earth and

rock were caked on it, revealing only a man-sized portion to the air. The jewel's pulsations went into a frenzy, beating faster and faster until the light became a constant shimmer. Ox pawed at his ears and gave a whine.

"Hear that?" said Targa. A piercing whistle at the edge of her hearing was streaming from the air around them. "Where is it coming from?"

The unearthly sound built in volume, making the cavern vibrate. Stalactites trembled and cracked off, crashing to the floor. "A cave-in!" Ox bleated.

Trebuchet waved the gemstone gently back and forth in front of the metal wall, oblivious to the noise. Along the surface, rock began to shred and crack, breaking apart into dust to reveal more and more of the dull, steely wall.

As abruptly as it had begun, the sound faded away, and the dust settled in the gloom. Leadbelly took a cautious step forward to examine the metal; a strip ten feet high and more than thirty feet long had been revealed.

He tapped it lightly. "Incredible. I think my initial estimations of the size of this chamber may have been too conservative." The scientist peered owlishly through his spectacles at the surface. "There appears to be a set of markings here. Circles and discs connected by thick lines. Dots and dashes, almost."

Trebuchet cupped the jewel in his hands and

threw back his head. "Ha! Have you ever seen the like?" He shouldered Leadbelly out of the way. "Since I was a child, I have always wanted to say this," he beamed. *"Open Sesame!"*

Targa blinked; for a second, she thought her eyes had deceived her. No doorway could be visible in the faultless metal wall, no edge or hinge visible – but then the steel seemed to run like hot wax off a candle, melting into itself to form an oval opening wide enough to admit two men side-by-side. Her amazement drew her closer and she studied the surface. It appeared as if the hole had been there all along. "What is this?" she hissed.

Leadbelly closed his mouth with a snap. "A higher science," he said, after a moment. "A far higher science."

Trebuchet stepped into the chamber without hesitation, taking the azure glow of the jewel with him. His head peeked back out at them.

"Coming?" he smiled.

Tyler crouched in the shadows as the rickety lift came to a sudden halt. He hadn't expected anyone to ride back up, and hesitated as a half-dozen workers, some running, some shuffling, poured out of the elevator.

"Hey, you!" He grabbed one of them, a young Indian boy from the Chinook nation. "What's happening down there?"

The lad stared at him, wild-eyed. "Evil!" he cried. "Get out while you can!" The boy struggled free of his grip and broke into a run.

Tyler cursed and examined the hoist; it seemed a simple enough mechanism...

"Put your hands up." The words were punctuated with the click of a hammer being cocked. Tyler did as he was ordered and turned to see Fivehawk and Rivercloud, both facing him with weapons drawn.

"Oh dear," he managed. "Look, I can explain..."

Rivercloud's eyes flashed with anger. "Tell me it is not true, white man. Tell me that you did not help the intruders steal The Heart."

Tyler stared at his feet. "I can't."

The woman slapped him hard across the face. "Betrayer! Fivehawk trusted you, I trusted you – and you gave us up!"

"I had no choice!" Tyler grated. "I was so damn angry when you people wouldn't help us mount a rescue, I tried alone and got captured for my stupidity."

Fivehawk's gun wavered a little, but he kept his aim on the cowboy.

"Trebuchet threatened to murder my uncle unless I helped him find the valley. What could I have done? He's the only family I have!"

Rivercloud felt her anger subside a little; she saw truth in Tyler's eyes, and the torture he was going through for abusing their trust.

"I was going to play along until I got Bill out, then get the jewel back to you. I never had any intention of letting them keep it. You gotta believe me!"

"I'm not sure," Fivehawk said levelly. "You willingly allied yourself with Drache's outriders — with The Faceless."

"Every second we stand here debating it, Trebuchet's down there in the pit doing who knows what with that bauble. I'm not your enemy. Give me a chance to prove it."

"How can we be certain you're not an outrider now?" asked Rivercloud.

Fivehawk holstered his gun and drew his knife. "I know a way." He tossed the blade to Tyler. "Hold the edge in your hand and squeeze it."

Tyler nodded grimly and did so, wincing as the blade bit into his palm. Blood oozed along the knife. He held it up to catch the light; crimson liquid flickered there.

"I still bleed red. I'm still me. Still the same old pigheaded Gabriel Tyler."

Rivercloud lowered her weapon. "You will have to repay the trust you broke."

"Let's start now, then." He entered the lift. "Going down. Next stop, basement."

Targa was the last to enter the metal chamber, and she cringed as she did, half expecting to step out into thin air and fall into a pit or catch herself in

140

some steel-lined death-trap. Instead, she felt an odd sense of dislocation, a weird texture in the air that made her feel unwelcome in this place — as if she were a square peg in a world of round holes. A glance to her left and right told her that Ox and Leadbelly felt the same way too. Only Trebuchet, with the jewel bouncing from hand to hand, seemed at home here.

"This place is creepy," Ox muttered.

"I quite agree," added Leadbelly. "The geometry of this architecture is very unsettling."

Targa turned in place to get a full look at the whole of the chamber's interior, and the sight of it made her head swim. What she could see of the room gave her the impression of a roughly circular space, perhaps sixty or a hundred yards across, with several curved spars of varying thickness extending from floor to ceiling. Soft white light glowed like will-o'-the-wisps from raised platforms around the middle of the room, an area sunk slightly into the floor like a miniature arena. The design was mirrored exactly on the roof, and Targa felt her footing wobble as she lost her balance for a second. It was like some bizarre funhouse, all sloping walls and funny angles that played tricks with the eyes. She had a sudden spark of understanding; as a child she'd once trapped a horsefly between two tin dinner plates and heard it buzz angrily about inside its disc-shaped prison. Now she was the fly, inside an oval chamber of metal.

"How could this be made?" she said aloud. "Who would drag all this steel plate down a mine and build a big metal room under the ground?" Targa stepped down into the centre of the antechamber, and the others followed. "It's the work of a madman."

Amazement bloomed on Leadbelly's face. "Good grief," he wheezed. "I don't think that's what happened at all."

"What do you mean, troll? How else could this be here? This must be some secret hiding place of Drache's, like a bank vault or something."

"I think this chamber may have been here for millions of years," he breathed.

"Millyuns?" Ox asked.

Targa made a dismissive noise. "Built for Drache by pixies and leprechauns, no doubt. You're such a bookworm, Leadbelly."

The scientist grunted. "At least I can read."

The woman began to snarl a response, but a loud "Ha!" from Trebuchet interrupted her. The Frenchman stood over a plinth in the middle of the room, slightly raised above all the others on a flat oval dais. "Look here. A keyhole for my beautiful key."

Trebuchet waved the stone over the head of the plinth and a ring of red light sprang into life on it.

Leadbelly cleared his throat. "I must insist you consider before proceeding. Master Drache was most emphatic that the contents of this chamber were highly dangerous – volatile, even. You saw how the jewel vibrated outside, you may cause an earthquake and kill us all. You must listen to me!"

Trebuchet rounded on the fat man, drawing his whip. The metallic cord quivered in the air, dancing of its own accord like a snake. "No," he raged, "*you* listen to *me*! Drache is not here and I am! I will open this vault and take his riches and then we will see who listens and does not listen!" With a tiny twist of the wrist, the whip shot out and snapped at the scientist. Leadbelly twisted away, the memory of Trebuchet's earlier attacks still fresh in his mind, but the whip impossibly altered course in mid-flight and snagged him around the leg. "Ox," he cried, "stop him!"

The weapon seemed to come alive, jerking itself from Trebuchet's hand and coiling around the portly little man. Ox and Targa watched, wide-eyed, as the whip's free end then turned and inserted itself into one of the smaller platforms. Leadbelly wailed as the whip reeled him in like a hooked fish until he was pressed flat against the wall, panting.

"Well," said Trebuchet. "I'm getting an inkling of what makes Drache so desperate to find this place that he'd risk the taint of the sky rock to get at it."

"It-it-it's alive!" Ox quailed, hesitating.

"Perhaps it is. What was it that Drache called it? That whip was a gift from our benefactor, the unseen, silent patron he communes with in his study..." He glanced at Targa. "I see it now, *cherie*. This is where those 'gifts' come from — this is our benefactor's storehouse of treasure!"

He hefted the jewel in one hand, and savagely thrust it into the ring of red light. "And now it's going to be mine!"

In the faded half-light of the chamber, none of the outriders had observed the three figures stealing through the doorway to hide behind one of the larger pillars.

"This place," Fivehawk whispered, "it carries the stench of ancient evil. The taint of The Faceless is strong here."

Tyler and Fivehawk exchanged confused glances as Trebuchet worked the jewel into the upper surface of the plinth.

"The Heart of the World!" Rivercloud hissed. "What is he doing to it?"

"Holy Cats! More to the point," said Tyler, "what is it doing to him?"

The plinth in front of Trebuchet blasted the chamber with a sunrise of white light, beams strobing out from the panel to hit the columns and platforms on the floor and the ceiling. The chamber resonated, the air vibrating with energy.

Fivehawk squinted through the brightness, trying to draw a bead on Trebuchet, ignoring the rattling of his teeth and the sudden aches in his head. He fired;

the bullet emerged from the gun barrel in slow motion, came to a halt and dropped, spent, a few inches from his hand.

"I've got bad feeling about this," husked Tyler.

Fivehawk's shot had not even been noticed by any of the outriders, their attention fixed on Trebuchet. The Frenchman had time for a whoop of triumph before a stream of red light bolted from the plinth and struck him in the face, knocking him to the floor like a roundhouse punch.

Rivercloud turned her head away to face the walls of the chamber and gasped; the featureless metal was shifting and flowing like water, shimmering into patterns that meant nothing to her, incomprehensible waves of rods and discs, page after page of angular symbols in riotous profusion. She screwed her eyes tight shut and held on to Fivehawk.

The rage of light ceased as quickly as it had begun, but now the interior of the chamber was aglow with a pinkish-red energy, a dull inferno colour that danced over the impossible walls and ceiling in uncomfortable patterns. Targa shook off her shock and backed away, leaving Ox still rigid with terror. Leadbelly grabbed uselessly at her from his whipcord prison.

"Help me!" he cried. "It's choking me!"

"Help yourself, fat man," she answered harshly. "I've seen enough of this madness!"

"Madness?" Trebuchet's voiced seemed to emerge from the walls and the very air itself. "On the contrary, *cherie*, I have never been more sane in my life."

The tall, thin Frenchman staggered to his feet and brushed imaginary dust from his jacket. "Ah," he managed. "I fell down."

A chill ran down Targa's spine. Whatever stood before her was not the short-tempered French whip-master she'd grown to know and loathe during her time in Drache's services – he had *changed*. It was as if someone with no proper idea of how a human being should look had made one from a vague description; all the features were there, it was recognizably Trebuchet, but re-drawn and rendered like the cruel-faced angels she recalled from Sunday School sermons of fire and brimstone. He was taller, thinner, his face lengthened into sharp planes of bone and skin, eyes reduced to snake-slits, lips like red razor blades. Trebuchet's limbs were wiry, and his hands – his awful, inhuman hands – ended in gaunt fingers with too many joints.

"I can taste you, Targa, like a scent on the wind." His voice had a hollow tone. "I see hate and fear and fear and hate. Poor, poor Targa." Trebuchet stepped around the plinth, testing his new limbs experimentally. "*Mon dieu!* Look at me!"

Ox's tiny mind reeled at the events around him. He wasn't a smart man; he had been slow and dumb since childhood, only finding enjoyment in inflicting pain on others. His time as an outrider, recruited by Rattler from a Mexican prison, had been his finest — he didn't need to think about anything except how to hurt people, and that had been fine. But now, this apparition that looked like the Frenchie, the funny fireworks and all the strange walls that made him feel sick, all of it hammered on him and broke something in his soft little brain. He roared like his bovine namesake and launched himself at Trebuchet.

The Frenchman watched him crash across the intervening two yards with cold detachment. When he was a foot away, Trebuchet held up his hands and tensed. His fingers extended like bony poles, eight points shooting bullet-fast in through Ox's chest and out of his back. They curved back on themselves and spread apart, slashing through flesh and muscle. Ox split open like a sack of meat and disintegrated, falling to the floor in a shower of black ash.

Targa saw her chance and bolted, diving through the open doorway and into the cavern beyond. She was in the elevator and ascending before Trebuchet had even noticed she was missing. He made a tutting noise.

Only a thin wailing from Leadbelly broke the silence. Fivehawk, Tyler and Rivercloud looked on from their hiding place in horror. A memory fluttered at the inside of Fivehawk's mind — a dream, a nightmare of a place filled with dark tunnels and a man with whips for fingers. "I know this chamber – I know what this is…"

"Come out from there," said Trebuchet airily. "Come and join the good doctor and myself." He chuckled, a sound like glass breaking. "After all, there's no point in performing without an audience."

Behind him, The Heart of the World throbbed and pulsed on the plinth like a live thing.

10: EARTHQUAKE!

They stepped into the miasma of light and colour cast by the spinning jewel, Tyler and Fivehawk with their guns at the ready and Rivercloud clutching a tomahawk, her knuckles white around its shaft.

Trebuchet roared with laughter, a peculiar sound that echoed around the metallic chamber. "Oh, what sport! You've come to challenge me!"

"Stop him!" squealed Leadbelly from his prone position. "He's mad!"

Trebuchet waved languidly at the fat scientist. "Be silent, little man." In response, the silver cord trapping Leadbelly tightened and he shrieked in pain.

"You have no comprehension of what you have unleashed," said Fivehawk levelly. "Look at yourself! You are already being changed, destroyed by it!"

Trebuchet made a show of studying his hands. "Why, you're right..." he murmured with sudden conviction. "I must stop right now..." Then his face split in a smile that showed too many teeth. *Idiot!*

What kind of fool do you think I am? I have power now, power that you cannot believe! You think mere words would be enough to make me surrender it?"

Tyler's hands were sweaty around the butt of his Peacemaker. He'd seen the impossible moments earlier when Fivehawk's bullets had fallen out of the air, so he knew the gun was useless — but what else could he do? What other weapons did he have? He flashed a quick glimpse at the Indian's stoic expression. Incredible. It seemed to Tyler that the longer he was in Fivehawk's company, the stranger the things were that he saw — and now he was looking into the eyes of a warped creature that had only moments earlier been a man. The thought made him shiver. The French whip-master's outer form now matched the black soul within it.

Trebuchet studied him and smiled. "You are like glass, Gabriel Tyler. I see through you, I see your terror and your fear." He patted the jewel with one hand. "I have been granted dominion over the minds of men."

Tyler felt a sudden pressure in his skull, like a heavy head cold. Somehow, in some arcane and evil way the Frenchman was reaching into his mind with that stare, peeling back the layers of his thoughts like an onion. He covered his eyes. "Get outta my head, you circus freak!" Tyler fought back, imagining Trebuchet's face contorted in pain, his body on fire...

The Frenchman snarled and broke free. "You ignorant insect!" he bellowed. "How dare you try to match wits with me! I am a god to you now!"

Tyler spat angrily. "I know God," he growled. "And you ain't him."

"You have poisoned The Heart of the World!" Rivercloud broke in.

Trebuchet shrugged. "This?" He stroked the jewel fondly, running his long fingers over the plinth on which it rested. "This belongs here, you silly girl. Don't you understand? It was never yours to begin with."

"The Great Spirit gave my tribe The Heart! It was our sacred trust to protect—"

Trebuchet clapped his hands together and a flash of red light flared in the room. "You unenlightened savages know nothing! I pity you all, I really do. With one simple action, I have raised myself over all of you and discovered the truth." He sighed. "It's quite an uplifting experience."

"Yeah? Shame you'll have to kow-tow to your big boss Mister Drache when he comes back, huh?" Tyler gibed. "Reckon he's gonna be mighty angry when he sees you've been playing with his toys."

"To Hades with Drache!" Trebuchet roared, his face turning feral, eyes glowing like embers. "Curse him and his stinking train!" The Frenchman stepped forward and grabbed Rivercloud's arm; it was a credit to her bravery that the girl did not scream, and stood her ground. "You think he rules me?" Trebuchet spat, enraged. "He is nothing! Nothing! A mere puppet for the real power, a mouthpiece!"

Releasing the girl, he stalked past Leadbelly's cowering form and moved to one of the smaller platforms. "Do you want to see the true Master? The beast that he bends his knee to?" He slapped his palm on the panel. "Then see what I have seen!"

Red and white pulses of light blinked from the platform and spun out like Catherine wheels into the walls. The metal boundary shifted and rippled.

Tyler clutched at his forehead, reacting to a sudden stabbing pain; Fivehawk and Rivercloud were also affected. The agony increased and he cried out, the ache blinding him — and at once his mind was flooded with images, sounds, sensations.

— a headlong rush through an infinity of darkness —

— falling from the sky, splitting the clouds with the sound of the passage —

— something small and vital falling free, tumbling away out of reach, a gleaming blue jewel —

— trailing fire and crashing into the earth, into the desert, into this place —

— buried in the sand, sinking, sinking —

— a huge darkness struggling from the crater, a shapeless, formless thing —

— it stumbles away, the ground turning black in its footsteps, animals and plants, nature herself withering in its wake —

152

*– and then waiting, endless waiting for the return,
dying, slowly dying –*

Tyler heard a far-off screaming, and pressed his
hands over his ears to shut it out. The images faded
from his mind, leaving faint impressions of
memories, like a wisp of smoke. He coughed through
a ragged throat and realized it was he who had cried
out. "What kind of crazy hocus-pocus is this?"

He was on his knees on the chamber floor, with
Rivercloud and Fivehawk close by. Gingerly, they
helped each other to their feet, their minds rubbed
raw by the shock of the ordeal.

"Now do you see?" intoned Trebuchet.

"I do," said Fivehawk shakily. "This is the stone
prison that The Faceless was trapped in, the one that
the stars themselves made to exile it from the
heavens. From here it rode down to the earth, and
then escaped out into the world."

"The Faceless," said Trebuchet, trying out the
words. "Yes, I suppose that's as good a name as any."

Tyler shook his head angrily, trying to wash away
the stain of the thoughts Trebuchet had forced into
it. "You're insane, Frenchie! You think your stage
mesmerism and some magic lantern lights are going
to change all that?"

Trebuchet gave a hollow chuckle. "Ah, the last
refuge of a small and limited mind, trying to explain
away the unknown as trickery." The cruel humour
vanished from his face. "I was planning on making a

gift of you, but perhaps now I will use you as an object lesson instead..."

"Wh-what do you mean?" Leadbelly managed.

The Frenchman looked down at the portly man and arched an eyebrow. "Why, surely it is clear to a man of your learning, Doctor? I intend no less than to usurp the good Master Robur Drache from his place as the hand of – what did he call it, The Faceless? – and kill him. I will provide the creature with what it desires the most, starting with these two." He pointed to Tyler and Fivehawk.

"Nice to be wanted," Tyler whispered.

Trebuchet's eyes narrowed and he raised his hands. A crackle of energy, like heat lightning, flashed between them. "Now, I'm going to blow you apart, Gabriel Tyler. And when I am finished, I'll find your uncle and your little water-carrying friend and destroy them ..." he sucked in a breath and bared his teeth, "and for an encore, I will murder the tribe of the Hidden People with a single thought!"

"No!" Rivercloud's shout came at the same instant she threw her tomahawk, the small axe spinning end over end towards Trebuchet's face. He cocked his head and the blade drifted to a stop in mid-air, then fell to the floor.

"You savages really are very slow learners, are you not?" He sighed. "I see my choice was incorrect. You shall be the first to die."

It was as if Trebuchet held a piece of the sun in his

hands; the fragment of brilliant light set shadows jumping all over the chamber and, with a flick of his wrists, he fashioned it into a bolt of white energy that flashed towards Rivercloud.

Tyler moved without conscious thought, his body reacting on pure instinct. He leapt at Rivercloud, colliding with her and dashing her to the silver floor. Rivercloud flinched as Trebuchet's blast turned the air into ozone as it passed, the heat of it beating at her face. Tyler's impact sent her skidding to her knees across the slick metallic surface before she tumbled to a halt near the plinth. She blinked. Her tomahawk was just inches from her hand.

"Oh," said Trebuchet, brushing powdery dead skin off his hands. "How noble."

Tyler was very still. Fivehawk's stomach flipped over in revulsion at the cloying, horrid stink of burnt flesh in the air as he knelt by the gunslinger. The lightning had caught him edge-on, flash-flaming through his jacket and shirt. An ugly wound cut across Tyler's right breast and ribcage, but, impossibly, he was still alive. The cowboy's breathing was weak and shallow, his face as pale as paper.

Fivehawk tried to banish the sudden hope that flared in his mind, but it was too late. Trebuchet clapped slowly.

"Oh, well done, *mon brave*. But now I shall finish him off, yes?"

"No," said Rivercloud, "you won't."

Trebuchet spun on his heel and gave a monstrous, inhuman cry. Rivercloud was poised over the plinth, her tomahawk in her hand. Colour drained from the Frenchman's alien features. "You cannot! You would not dare to!"

Rivercloud recalled her father's words in her mind – *I swear by the Sacred Hoop, I will shatter it with my own bare hands before I allow the demon to possess it!* – and saw Trebuchet's terror as he read the intent in her thoughts. She brought the axe down with all her might on the jewel that sat on the plinth. The tomahawk blade bisected The Heart of the World with a sound like the sky breaking open, and the glowing blue gemstone shattered into hundreds of jagged bits.

Trebuchet's thunderous scream echoed around the chamber, making the walls tremble and shake, the floor shifting like the deck of a ship in high seas.

Fivehawk cradled Tyler's injured body and ran for the doorway, calling over his shoulder. "Run!"

Rivercloud sprinted after him, through the metal orifice and into the cave beyond.

Still restrained by the silver whipcord, Leadbelly cried out as she raced past him. "Save me! Don't leave me here! I'm sorry!"

Targa was running as fast as she could. The leather-clad woman shot from the mouth of the mine like a cork from a bottle, blinking and swearing as her eyes adjusted back to the daylight on the surface. She skidded to a momentary halt and made a sour face. All around her, the shacks and rough huts of the compound were either ablaze or collapsed heaps of broken beams and timber. In amidst the wreaths of smoke, Targa saw the braves on horseback racing back and forth, and the slaves fighting with the few remaining outriders. She spat and kicked at the dust.

The whole thing was falling to pieces; she'd let her greed get in the way of her good sense and now the mine was a ruin. Targa felt icy fear in her gut as she thought of Drache. He would return today and discover this failure, and in his blind rage he would no doubt kill her – or worse.

Ducking from cover to cover, she sprinted to one of the few shacks still standing. A horse, wide-eyed and spooked by all the gunfire and flames, struggled at a tether that held it to a hitching post. Targa calmed the animal and mounted it, all the time her eyes searching for an escape route.

She had it. She would ride out to intercept Drache early and spin him a tale about Trebuchet's treachery. *Yes, that's it*, she smiled to herself, *I tried to stop him, but he would not listen…* Targa tried on an expression of fear and sorrow and then laughed.

"You got nothing to be smiling about, *girlie*," said a voice behind her.

Targa turned her mount around and scowled. Tulsa stepped out in front of her, a rifle in her hands aimed at Targa's chest. "Reach for the sky, sister."

With a petulant snort, Targa did as she was ordered. "What do you expect to accomplish, wench? A slattern like you trying to take me in?"

Tulsa's face hardened. "I ought to kill you for what you've done to all these people here," she snarled, jerking her head to indicate the camp, "but I reckon you'll be swinging from a rope soon enough. Get off your horse. Slowly."

Targa's eyes narrowed. "Whatever you say," she said pleasantly.

Without warning, a shock rippled through the ground like a deep peal of thunder, shaking and rolling the earth. Targa's horse reared up on its hind legs and neighed; Tulsa struggled to keep her footing and lost her grip on the rifle.

Targa saw a chance and took it, flicking her wrist with a crack of leather. From a hidden pocket inside her sleeve, a slender glass knife emerged, a hollow blade filled with a yellowish liquid. The weapon dropped into her palm and she threw it hard at Tulsa. The shifting ground put off her aim and the knife struck the dirt and shattered, releasing the liquid to the air; the chemical reacted instantly and flashed into thick yellow smoke.

Tulsa's eyes flooded with tears as she fumbled for the rifle. Coughing, she loosed three shots after Targa as she galloped away, but the female outrider did not slow, racing up to the railhead and charging onward, following the rusted rails of the track into the hills.

Tulsa got to her feet and dusted herself down when the ground settled. She looked back towards the mine entrance. Was Tyler still alive down there? She feared that the brief tremor might have been from a cave-in or explosion underground – but in the next second her heart leapt into her mouth as the vibrations began anew, stronger and harder this time, ripples appearing in the sand as the land shuddered and cracked.

"Earthquake!" she cried to anyone in earshot.

Fivehawk supported Tyler's semi-conscious form with one arm, and grabbed at the pull-rope by the lift shaft. He tugged on it hard, but instead of the answering bell and the clatter of the descending cage, the cord came away in his hand. Rivercloud clutched at the end of the rope – it was cleanly severed, most likely by a knife blade.

"Targa," Fivehawk grated. "She's trapped us all down here." His voice barely carried over the ominous rumblings that came from all around them.

Their only illumination came from a guttering torch, casting yellow light across the shaking walls and catching streams of powdered rock as they cascaded from the ceiling. Fivehawk's stomach knotted in alarm as he imagined the cavern collapsing in on them, thousands of tons of stone and earth pressing down on their frail human bodies. He glanced over his shoulder at the metallic chamber. Random pulses of light were flashing out of the doorway, a sickly, cancerous red in colour; by shattering The Heart, Rivercloud had started the death throes of Trebuchet's power source.

A stalactite crashed to the floor near them, shattering into fragments. "We must climb!" Fivehawk shouted, gesturing to a ladder of rotting wood that followed the length of the shaft.

"Impossible!" Rivercloud cried. "You can't climb and carry Tyler as well!"

"I won't leave him behind!" Fivehawk said hotly.

"We would never reach the surface in time!" she added, and Fivehawk sagged inwardly. The woman was right; they had perhaps only moments before the cave-in began.

He sidestepped a stream of fist-sized stones that crashed out of the darkness. "Then we will die here..." he said, with grim finality.

"We will *not*!" Rivercloud yelled. "There is another way! Follow me!"

Fivehawk shifted Tyler's weight and ran after her, dodging between parts of the rocky roof as they fell in around him. She vanished into a dark passage that he had not noticed when they arrived.

"Lemme go..." wheezed Tyler faintly. "Leave me here and get out..."

"Shut up, Paleface," said Fivehawk firmly.

They entered the passageway and the Indian frowned. The floor sloped away, extending downward deeper into the earth instead of up towards the surface.

"Rivercloud!" he cried. "Where are you going?"

The torch flickered faintly ahead of him, and over the rumble of the turbulent earth, he caught a different sound, a rushing noise like wind ... or water.

"To the river!" came her voice. "Quickly!"

Trebuchet screamed like a wounded animal, his long-fingered hands clutching at the myriad fragments of broken jewel on the plinth before him. Absolute terror overwhelmed him and panic set in as he tried desperately to re-assemble The Heart of the World, trying to put the shattered shards into an order that would resemble the spherical gem. The glowing globe had been scattered all over the plinth by the blow from Rivercloud's tomahawk, and for every piece Trebuchet grabbed, an infinity of others, tiny as needles, was scattered out before him. He pressed his hands together, tears blinding him, and squeezed, channelling as much energy as he could into moulding the remnants into shape. His fingers parted and he threw back his head and wailed; instead of bonding them, he had caused the fragments to break apart into a fine, glittering powder, which drifted away through his fingers.

He staggered from the plinth, his mind reeling. The chamber was shaking like a rattle, the rippling metal walls now broken and covered with patterns like spider-webs. The identical floor and ceiling flexed in and out in a fearful rhythm.

"Ruined!" he screamed. "Ruined!"

On the floor, Leadbelly looked past Trebuchet to the plinth. The red glow that suffused it was shifting and changing, the steady heartbeat throb it emitted only moments ago now replaced with an inflamed, off-kilter pulsing. Great crackles of power flashed out to the walls and the floor like spurts of ball lightning.

Trebuchet took a step closer to Leadbelly and the scientist felt a shriek die in his throat, strangled by the sight of the outrider. The sharp, chiselled edges of his face were gone, and in their place was puckered, aged skin peeling away in thin wisps. Trebuchet's flesh clung to his bones, the hollow coves of his cheeks and eye-sockets turning black as blood pooled and congealed in them. Hair trailed off the Frenchman's head in dry clumps, taking shreds of dead, powdery epidermis with it. Trebuchet was a walking corpse, a collection of bony angles in a split bag of skin.

"Oh, please," Leadbelly quailed, finding his voice. "Please release me!"

"Release you?" Trebuchet's voice was breathy and sibilant. "Of course."

With a final exercise of his power, Trebuchet waved his hand and the steely whipcord around Leadbelly's body undulated, suddenly sprouting barbs all along its length like the stem of a rose. "Release," he said quietly, and the cord tore into the fat man, chopping through his stomach, torso and neck, opening Leadbelly like a sack of offal.

The effort had drained Trebuchet and he staggered back to the plinth, stepping through the yellow-green ashes of Leadbelly's corpse as the fat scientist dissolved. Something fell from his face and landed on the floor with a wet splat. He held up a hand to his head and howled; his hawkish nose had torn away from his skin. Even as Trebuchet watched, great curls of flesh and muscle began to slough off his hands, falling to the ground in hissing heaps of pinkish-grey matter, leaking olive-coloured blood in thin streams. He opened his mouth to scream and a rain of teeth escaped, tiny white stones blackening as they dislodged from his gums.

The plinth vibrated and shook, the scarlet pulses within it strobing at incredible speed; Trebuchet had only a moment to force a breath of air out through his disintegrating throat before the plinth vanished in a column of red energy. A shock wave of light flashed out across the chamber, rebounding off the walls and striking the point from which it came. Trebuchet's body and the remnants of Leadbelly flashed out of existence, consumed in its wake.

And then the column broke open, revealing the source of the chamber's power, an impossibly perfect sphere of naked energy, a dark disc escaping its cage. The chamber imploded, dragged into the sphere in a flash of light, followed by tons of rock and stone. The earth cried out and shook.

They emerged into a cavern split by a racing underground stream. Fivehawk hesitated as he realized the rushing water was only coming up for air here, and no doubt continued for miles through tunnels of rock.

"We can't swim through this!" he yelled. "We'll be dashed to shreds on the rapids, and Tyler will drown!"

Rivercloud's face was defiant. "The river spirit will protect us! Trust me! There is no other way!" Before he could even begin to argue, she leapt from the stone bank and dived headfirst into the white water.

The earth and rock around them began to shiver like a struck drum-skin. Grasping a handful of Tyler's belt, Fivehawk sucked in a lungful of air and held the gunslinger to him.

"Hey," Tyler managed groggily. "Where we goin'?"

"For a swim," said the Indian, and pulled him into the icy grip of the underground river.

11: THE BROKEN LAND

The slave workers and the braves from the Hidden People felt the ground tremble beneath their feet, and they ran, scattering in all directions from the epicentre of the earthquake. Hundreds of feet below the surface, ancient strata of rock that had lain undisturbed for millennia now shattered and broke apart, collapsing in on each other and re-arranging the geology of the mine like the ingredients in a cocktail shaker. If an observer could have hovered high above the compound, they would have seen an awesome sight as a ring of tremors radiated out from the mine entrance like the ripples on a pond cast by a thrown stone, sending a wave of dirt and earth outward across the plain. The few buildings still standing were upset and broken apart by the shock wave's passage, timbers thrown into the air like a handful of giant matchsticks. The single track of railroad that flanked the mine camp was twisted and bent, warped into a crazy curve of metal. In the wake of the tremor, the ground dropped by several yards, creating a vast shallow crater.

For a moment, the tortured earth fell silent, and some of the running figures escaping the quake skidded to a halt and thanked the fates that the ordeal was over; but in the next second they were screaming and running again, as a mighty roar vibrated up through the ground like the sound of a waking monster. In the place deep below where the metal chamber had resided, now only the dark sphere of energy remained, unleashed by Trebuchet's folly. The shimmering globe rippled as it struggled to consume the stone and earth around it, casting great flashes of light as it was overwhelmed. With one last effort, the sphere collapsed in on itself with a catastrophic detonation. The chamber and the secrets that it held, the answers to questions about the true nature of The Faceless, were reduced instantly to atoms as the ground rose up to meet the sky, tearing a vast hole in the desert.

Fivehawk fought the reflex to expel all the air in his lungs as he struck the icy waters of the underground river. As soon as he entered the current, his arms clutching Tyler to him, all sensation and feeling became meaningless. There was no way to know where or how he was moving, no markers or reference points to see or hear. The water was like liquid darkness, smothering him in a freezing embrace that reached through clothes, through skin and muscle right down to the very marrow of his bones. They tumbled and bobbed through the stone channels of the river, the rage of the water projecting them through narrow arteries cut in the bedrock by thousands of years of flowing streams. The currents buffeted and turned them, bouncing them off the tunnel walls, spinning and spiralling them, and always pushing them on, faster and faster.

Fivehawk's chest began to burn with the effort of holding in his breath, and he expelled the air little by little, trying to measure and wring every last moment of oxygen from his lungs – but still the headlong plunge continued. The Indian felt fear surround him as his mind opened itself to the terror of the cold, wet darkness. What if they were plunging deeper and deeper into the earth, never to emerge into the air? What if Rivercloud was already dead, ripped apart by jagged stone teeth somewhere ahead? Fivehawk's hands were numb and unresponsive. A thought flashed through him – he could no longer feel his grip on Tyler's body! He had let the semi-conscious gunslinger go, to tumble through the frenzied waters and vanish.

His head bounced off a rock outcrop and lit firework flashes of pain in his skull, blasting the last ergs of energy from his chilled body. Fivehawk could no longer struggle and faded into the dark, smothered by the infinite inky void of the cold, cold river.

*   *   *

Tons of earth were catapulted into the air, blocking out the sun and casting huge ruddy clouds across the sky. Some of those who fled fell to their knees and wept, praying for deliverance as the heavens turned black above them, fearing that Judgement Day had come.

From the ridge line, Looks-Far chanced a glance back at the place where the mine compound had once been, where now a bowl of shredded, broken land sat, dotted with tiny fires and scattered scraps of wood. His heart hammered in his chest as fear gripped him, in part afraid that some huge beast would suddenly emerge from the dirt, but mostly dreading the awful thought that his beloved Rivercloud was crushed somewhere under that vast, earthen blanket. As he watched, the black volcanic hummocks of the Burnt Hills themselves seemed to shudder, and slowly they sank into the dirt, the series of dark bluffs caving in and collapsing into the vast wounds gashed in the ground. In moments, the sooty hillside was gone, replaced by cracked flatlands. As if they had never been there.

Looks-Far had little time to marvel at the turmoil of the earth. His horse, already skittish in the extreme and barely under his control, struggled against his reins and foamed at the mouth with exertion. He sensed what was troubling the beast a moment later; the tremors had reached the ridge where he stood, and the ground flexed. The brave spurred his horse on and the animal bolted. He did not chance another look back, and so did not see the entire ridge drop by several yards. Instead, Looks-Far saw the ground and sky suddenly switch places as the final aftershock of the earthquake raced outwards, pitching him off his horse and throwing both rider and mount to the shuddering sands.

The river emerged several miles away from the Burnt Hills, in a kidney-shaped lake that nestled at the bottom of a steep-walled arroyo. The flow of water forced an endless series of gentle, lapping waves to break on the lakeside, and this action deposited three gasping humans half-in and half-out of the water, resting on a tiny stretch of pebbled beach. Rivercloud shook off the chill first and pulled the injured Tyler to safety, then slapped the colour back into Fivehawk's cheeks to rouse him. Miraculously, the gunslinger was awake, although his breathing was still shallow and laboured. He managed a wan smile.

"Feel like I been rode hard and put away wet," he wheezed, spitting up a mouthful of riverwater. He gingerly poked at the wound on his torso. "Ouch."

Fivehawk mouthed silent thanks to the spirits of the river and the lake, then lay on his back, panting. He felt the dying shivers of the earthquake through the rocky beach.

"I know this place," said Rivercloud. "We are at

the edge of our territories, but still within walking distance of the valley."

Fivehawk glanced at Tyler. "Can you walk?"

The gunslinger made a poor attempt at covering up his pain. "Sure I can."

"We will rest a while," the Indian said firmly.

Rivercloud left them and wandered away, searching the edges of the steep rocky cliffs for a path. The two men exchanged long, silent glances as she walked out of earshot, both mulling over the past few days' events.

Tyler broke the silence. "I guess I owe you an apology."

"For stealing The Heart?" Fivehawk said. "What you did was wrong, but I confess that I might have done the same."

"For your sister?"

Fivehawk nodded. "You are fortunate, Tyler, to have found your uncle. I fear I may never see my sister again."

"There were lots of Indians in the camp," said Tyler, with a little eagerness. "She could be one of them."

Fivehawk shook his head. "No. If she were here, I would know it."

"Then, maybe one of them might know where she is…"

A tiny flicker of hope danced in Fivehawk's heart. "Perhaps," he said, allowing himself a moment of optimism.

Tyler removed his jacket and shirt with exaggerated slowness and started to wring the water from them. "Anyhow, that's not what I meant. When I said I was sorry."

"I don't understand." Fivehawk got to his feet and took up a length of fallen branch, stripping the bark from it.

"When we rode to Stonetree and rescued those folks, I saw men that bled green blood, and a fellow walking through flames even though I'd shot him dead a moment before, and here I saw a man change into ..." he paused, and shuddered, "into *something*. Now you've been telling me that this is all some magical hocus-pocus, demons and all that boojum, and I ain't been believing it."

"Has what you've seen today, in that chamber, changed your mind?"

"I'm still not sure, but I'll tell you this. I'm sorry that I doubted you. I guess you were right when you told me once there are things in the world that are outside anything I've ever seen or heard of." He smiled and tore off a strip of his shirt to fashion a makeshift bandage, flinching in pain as he dressed the wound. "One thing that can't be questioned – whether I believe in these demons of yours or not, they sure hurt like hell when they're trying to kill you."

Fivehawk handed Tyler the branch, which he had made into a rough-hewn crutch. "Here, this will help you walk."

Rivercloud called from the foot of the cliffs, waving.

"She's found the route outta here," said Tyler, shifting his weight. "Time to head back and face the music, I guess."

Fivehawk nodded. "I will explain to Grey Arrow—"

Tyler cut him off. "No. You put yourself on the line for me once with these people, but not again. I'm taking the blame this time."

Doggedly, he walked away, resting on the crutch as he did so. Fivehawk nodded to himself and followed.

The climb was a long and slow one, and the day was waning into late afternoon by the time they reached the top of the steep cliffs. For a moment, Fivehawk was confused by the sight laid out before him, disoriented by the landscape.

"This is wrong... There is the mesa of the Painted Cave," he breathed, pointing into the distance, "but the hills – where are the hills?"

"Gone," said Rivercloud simply. "The earth has swallowed them whole."

Tyler nodded. "Good riddance, I say."

Eventually they reached the site of the mine and found more evidence of the fate of the Burnt Hills. The camp had vanished as if it had never been there, replaced by a shallow, perfectly oval valley. The ground was uneven and undulated gently, like wave-tops frozen in time and rendered into dark earth.

"It seems that the ground has renewed itself," Rivercloud noted.

Here and there broken pieces of wood were dotted around; Fivehawk nudged one lengthy segment with his boot and recognized it as a part of the roof from one of the guard towers.

"Hey!" called Tyler. "Look at this!"

Rivercloud and Fivehawk walked over to where the cowboy stood. Tyler pointed at the ground before them with his crutch. In a small lee of the valley, a stream was running. "That wasn't there before."

"It must have been pushed up to the surface after the shock, the earthquake."

Rivercloud took in the landscape and sighed. "This is good land, rich and fertile now."

"You would never know what happened here," Tyler added.

"I wonder..." Fivehawk said, dropping to his haunches. "What became of the sky rock the miners dug up?"

"Hey, yeah!" Tyler brightened. "We sure could use some of that stuff, in case Drache turns up."

Rivercloud pointed to a lonely spar of steel poking up from the earth a way distant, a mute monument to the tracks that had been buried by the quake. "The railroad the white man laid here was not spared. No one will come this way unless they travel by horse."

Fivehawk cupped a handful of dirt and let it fall away through his fingers. He chuckled to himself. "Look here. Here is our sky rock."

Tyler and Rivercloud studied the thin streams of dirt. Sunlight seemed to twinkle off them as they cascaded from Fivehawk's hand.

"What's that? Gold dust, or something? Copper from the mine?"

Fivehawk shook his head, and held out his hand palm up. A little pile of dirt remained, and mixed in it were sparkles of jade green, almost too tiny to be seen.

"Well, I'll be damned," said Tyler. "Sky rock dust?"

"The stores of the stone they excavated must have been caught in the upheaval and shattered into powder. The quake scattered it all over this area."

"Salted the ground with it," Tyler said ruefully. "Well, at least one good thing comes from that."

"What would that be?" asked Rivercloud.

"Whoever lives here from now on will never be troubled by the outriders again. That stone is like poison to them."

Hoof-beats drew their attention away; riders from the Hidden People approached, weapons at the ready, wary of attack. The lead rider's face split in a smile when he recognized Rivercloud.

"You're safe!" he exclaimed. "We feared the worst when the earth became angry."

"Where are the people from the prison of earth?"

she asked, sensing the question preying on the minds of Tyler and Fivehawk.

"They have come to the valley," said the brave, in a tone that suggested he only half-believed his own words.

"But how?" Rivercloud asked. "How could they find it?"

"We are Hidden no longer," the brave replied.

They rode with the warriors back to the valley as the sun dipped towards the horizon. As they reached the mesa, the brave's words made sense. They saw that the towering mesa itself had not been spared the wrath of the quake, shedding parts of itself into dry heaps of rust-coloured rock at the foot of the butte. Fivehawk noted that the mouth of the Painted Cave, hardly visible to the naked eye on a clear day, was now choked with rubble. That entrance would never be open again.

The brave broke the long silence of the ride as they passed around the mesa towards the towering stone walls that stood sentinel over the secret valley. "The Hidden People have been found."

All three of them gasped at the sight that stood before them. Where before there had been a sheer, unclimbable rockface, now there was nothing but a pile of boulders. The wall that separated the green canyon had fallen away, forever opening the home of the Hidden People to the world outside.

"The earthquake must have knocked the valley wall down," Tyler whispered.

"Perhaps," said Rivercloud. "Or perhaps there is another reason."

They dismounted with the warriors and made their way towards the valley. Tyler pulled on Fivehawk's arm and pointed. Close by, a rough congregation of battered wagons and tents were camped out, and the ragged escapees from the mine sat or stood around with guarded, suspicious looks on their faces.

"They need food and water," Fivehawk noted. "But they are afraid to approach the valley and ask for it."

Tyler looked back at the Indians. "And these folks, they don't trust strangers." The cowboy hesitated for a moment, wanting to approach the ex-prisoners and see if his uncle was with them. "No," he said aloud. "First things first."

As well as he could, Tyler walked into the valley with Fivehawk and Rivercloud beside him. Looks-Far was guarding the entrance with a dozen more braves and he whooped with joy when he saw the girl's face. Ignoring protocol, he rushed to her and swept her off her feet, kissing her.

"Looks-Far!" she said, only half in anger. "You forget your manners!"

"I care not," he replied with feeling. "All I care about is you."

And for the first time in her life, Rivercloud was struck speechless.

Tyler's welcome was far colder, however. Looks-Far's face turned red with anger. "You!" he snarled. "You dare show yourself here!" The brave's pistol was suddenly in his hand, inches from Tyler's chest. "It is because of you that The Heart of the World was stolen!"

Fivehawk and Rivercloud both shouted "No!" but it was Grey Arrow's hand that held Looks-Far back. The Elder paused a moment to embrace his daughter, and then turned to face Tyler. The old Indian's expression was as dark as a storm cloud.

"You and your kind are not welcome here," he said, with barely controlled anger. "Leave now."

"Not before I clear the air," said Tyler. "I was the one responsible for the theft of your jewel, I and I alone."

Amazement vibrated through the assembled tribespeople. "You admit such a crime?" Looks-Far growled.

"I do. I did it because I thought it was the only way to save my own family from death. I was going to return it to you ... but I know that is no excuse for what I did. I'll take whatever punishment you'll give."

"Young Paleface," Grey Arrow began carefully, "you show honour and candour for answering to your crime, and that I respect. I understand the bonds of blood will force us to do things we do not wish to –" he looked meaningfully at his daughter – "but know this. Our sacred laws have only one punishment for this transgression."

"Death!" barked Looks-Far, ready to carry out the sentence.

"How do you answer now, Paleface?" The Elder grated.

Tyler licked at dry lips, the pain in his side increasing into a steady burning. "I ... that is..." He paled. "I ask your forgiveness. I did what I thought was right, but I am sorry. My uncle taught me to take responsibility for all my actions, and if that means I have to face death, then bring it on."

Tyler let the crutch drop to the dirt and drew himself up to his full height. His face was pallid and his breath came in gasps, but he stood proudly. "If that's what it's gotta be, then ... then..." Like a puppet with its strings cut, Tyler abruptly collapsed in a heap. Fivehawk rushed to him, opening his jacket. The bandage around his torso was slick with blood and infection.

"Oh, no," Fivehawk whispered. "His injuries are worse than I realized. He is close to death."

"Perhaps the Great Spirit has judged him for us," Looks-Far nodded.

"Father!" Rivercloud shouted. "Tyler's guilt must be forgiven! He saved my life when the demon was about to murder me — he redeemed himself for stealing The Heart, and I did as you said, destroying it to keep it from the great enemy!"

Fivehawk nodded. "It is true. Tyler risked himself to save Rivercloud's life. If he dies now, it will be so that she could live."

Grey Arrow knelt over Tyler, tracing a hand over the wound in his chest. "My daughter lives because of this man?" The old man hesitated, his expression softening. "Then perhaps that may be redemption enough. If this Tyler's heart is strong enough to fight the minions of The Faceless, I am sure the Great Spirit would not wish him dead." He glanced up at Fivehawk. "Not if he still has a part to play in the coming battle." With a sharp gesture, the elder summoned a group of squaws and a shaman. "This paleface may yet still live. Take him to the healing lodge and care for him. If he dies, it will not be by the hand of our people." When the tribespeople hesitated, he barked out an order. "Quickly! I command it!"

Looks-Far rounded on Grey Arrow. "Elder, have you lost your mind? The palefaces are all our enemies, just like every intruder!" He gestured towards the makeshift camp outside the valley. "See how even now they wait and plot to steal our lands? We have lost The Heart to them and now they will take our very lives!"

"Those people are not plotting against you, they are afraid and lonely!" Fivehawk broke in. "They have been prisoners on your territory for months while you did nothing to help them!" He jabbed a finger in Looks-Far's chest. "They have nothing but need, and yet you would turn your back on them, paleface and redskin alike, rather than help them." Fivehawk looked at the tribespeople all around him as he spoke. "The Great Spirit teaches us that all things are part of the whole, no matter where they come from. If you cast hate on them, you become no different to the outriders who attacked you!"

"But it is our way—" said Looks-Far, suddenly unsure of himself.

"Then our way must change!" Rivercloud interrupted. "Ask yourself, why has the wall fallen? Why has our exile from the world come to an end?"

"All things that are, are the wish of the Great Spirit," Grey Arrow said with a nod. "We were tasked to guard The Heart of the World until the day it was needed. Perhaps that day was today."

"Then our secret valley is no longer secret ... because our duty has been fulfilled?" Looks-Far's face reflected the turmoil in his mind. "But if that is so, then what are we to do now?"

Fivehawk's anger ebbed away. "You must seek a new duty, Looks-Far."

The brave hesitated a moment, then, with a simple gesture, he dropped the heavy gun in his hands to the dirt and stepped out of the valley. He turned to face Grey Arrow, his eyes lit from within by new understanding. "With your permission, Elder, I should like to bring some ..." he frowned, searching his thoughts for the right word, "some *guests* into our valley."

The Elder looked at his daughter and nodded. "Yes. The isolation of the Hidden People is over. It's time to bring the outside world in."

Rivercloud hugged her father and as Fivehawk watched, Looks-Far and the other braves escorted the escaped slave workers into the valley, the suspicion and tension on their faces gradually giving way to gratitude and relief.

12: FOLLOW THE SUN

It was as if the quake had unleashed a strange energy on the earth around the Burnt Hills mine; like the tingle in the air that follows a thunderstorm, the territory the Indians had renamed The Broken Land was alive with vitality. In places where only rock and scrub had survived before, now plants were sprouting. Nature had shrugged off the yoke of the outriders and been reborn.

The tribe – they no longer called themselves the Hidden People – took to their new friends quickly, following Rivercloud's example. As Tyler healed, Fivehawk watched the diverse groups come together and bond. Many of the former prisoners were malnourished, some even as close to death as poor Gabriel had been, but the tribe had food to spare and they grew to enjoy giving. Within a few weeks, groups of the escapees began to trickle away from the valley, heading home to families and friends that most likely thought them dead, still sworn to keep the secrets of the valley. A few men and women from Stonetree set off back across the scrubland to their town, but Tyler's uncle stayed on, as well as the girl who called herself Tulsa.

Some of the prisoners were Indians. Fivehawk walked among their encampment noting braves and squaws, even children, from nations far and wide across the lands. He felt a curious mingling of emotions, sadness and joy chief among them. In part, the sight hardened his resolve to hunt down and stop Drache and The Faceless, to put an end to an evil that could enslave innocents from tribes scattered across the entire continent, but it also gave him pause as he considered the very size and reach of Drache's empire. He'd learnt from Tyler that Robur Drache was a ruthless industrialist and rail baron, and he had no doubt that Drache's dealings with the demon had been a perfect match in intent and evil. As he looked from face to face, he could not help but hope against hope that one would turn up to gaze at him with his sister's perfect smile; but she was not here. He had known that ever since they had first sighted the mine on their arrival. She was still lost, waiting for him to find her.

A hand tugged on his arm, bringing him out of his reverie. Rivercloud gave him a concerned look. "Wanderer, I called your name twice but you did not seem to hear me. Are you unwell?"

He shook his head, forcing a smile. "No. I was just ... thinking about someone."

Rivercloud saw the distant pain in his eyes and

gave his arm a comforting squeeze. "There is someone you should meet, Fivehawk. A boy. Come with me."

She led him through a line of tepees to a trio of Apaches, two lean women and a teenage boy. "This is Tall Tree," she said, indicating the youth. "He knows of your sister."

It was all Fivehawk could do not to grab the boy and shake the information out of him then and there; instead he sat carefully and fixed him with a hard stare. Tall Tree matched his gaze measure for measure – there was no guile in his eyes.

"I knew a Wanderer woman," he piped. "She protected me when the overseers wanted to whip me for being insolent." The boy managed a smile. "She made me laugh when the outriders were not around. She has eyes like yours."

"Her name –" Fivehawk began, stumbling over the words, hardly able to bring voice to them. "Her name is Eyes-Like-Amber."

Tall Tree clapped his hands together and grinned. "Amber! She was Ulanutani like you, strong like the tree but gentle like rain." His face fell. "But she went away."

"Away? Where?" Fivehawk felt his every sense become alert, on edge, as it would when he was hunting. He knew he had to capture every last morsel of information from this child if he were to seek his sister. "Where did she go?"

"The fat paleface, the one with the face of a pig, came one day and took many of us away. Some came back, but many did not. Eyes-Like-Amber did not come back."

"They took them out on the iron road." One of the Apache women spoke for the first time. "Shackled them like dogs, put them into wagons and the metal horse took them away, to the far north."

"To another place? Another mine, like the Burnt Hills?" Fivehawk struggled to keep desperation out of his voice. To find a lead like this boy and then to discover it led nowhere ... that would be more than he could take.

"Some of the other prisoners have spoken about the one you called Drache?" Rivercloud said. "Of the hairless head and dark glass eyes?" Fivehawk nodded, and she continued, "A Kiowa brave told me of rumours he heard around the camp, that Drache had ordered his outriders to recruit slaves to work on a railroad. Your sister was likely taken there."

Fivehawk mumbled thanks to the Apaches and stepped away, his mind conflicted. He found himself at the newly created entrance to the valley, and stood there a while, looking out at the mesas beyond. Sunlight flared off something bright in the distance – part of the mine's rail spur.

His jaw hardened. *A sign, old Grandfather?* he wondered, his thoughts turning to Sleeping Fox, the aged shaman who had started him on his journey, in what seemed like a lifetime ago. *Once again, you show me my path.*

Fivehawk felt a clearness return to his thoughts, a subtle strength suffuse him. He felt refreshed; his purpose had been renewed. At last, after months of wondering and fearing the worst, the Indian knew his sister was alive. "I will find you," he said to the air. "I will break your chains with my bare hands." And yet, a part of him felt sorrow. For Tyler, the quest had ended. With his Uncle Bill rescued from the clutches of the outriders, Gabriel Tyler's reason for riding with Fivehawk had vanished. The white man had what he had sought, and even though the prophecy that Sleeping Fox had described spoke of two men's mission to stop The Faceless, Fivehawk knew that he could not force Tyler to travel any further. It would be his choice to make, and if Fivehawk found himself alone, then that would be the way of it. He sighed, and sank to his knees to watch the sun set.

Time had passed in a blur for Tyler, the days turning into weeks as he slipped in and out of wakefulness, until at last his body began to regain its strength. He had grown tired of the healing lodge almost as soon as he was able to sit up on the rough mattress of blankets and grasses the squaws had provided him. He grumbled at the shaman as the old man applied cures from his medicine bundle, but not too much, recalling how Fivehawk had helped heal a bullet wound he had suffered on the occasion of their first meeting on the road to Whiteford. Part of him had been surprised to wake up at all, expecting to take a shot through the heart for his admission of theft, but a visit from Rivercloud, who brightened his mood with her smiles, explained how his selfless act of heroism in saving her life had – after much debate and not a few cross words – granted him forgiveness.

Tyler had allowed himself a grin. "I guess that was kinda heroic of me, wasn't it? Some might even say noble."

She told him about the curious change that had swept over the territory, not just over the land itself, but the people. She seemed sure that many of the displaced ex-slaves, especially those from the Indian nations, were planning to stay a while, and maybe even stay for ever. Thanks in part to his impulsiveness, the Hidden People were no more, he realized with a pang of sadness, but Rivercloud told him that although the deeds had been his, it was the Great Spirit that caused them to happen. He smiled. That made him feel a little better. Heck, even Looks-Far had grudgingly sneaked into the lodge the night before and thanked him, albeit through gritted teeth.

His companions for the most part were Uncle Bill and Tulsa, who visited him once or twice a day, chatting about the valley and just generally being glad to be free once more. Tulsa was always guarded about her past, but Tyler had learnt enough to know she had fallen into Drache's clutches after leaving home to drift across the West in search of fortune. Bill had warmed to the girl and promised her a place to stay, and the chance for a fresh start, back in Stonetree, which she gingerly accepted.

Only one person hadn't come to see him – Fivehawk. Tulsa told him that the Indian had been combing the escapee camp for information about Drache's operation, and Tyler felt a vague pang of guilt in his chest, as if he knew he should be helping in some way. But his search had ended the moment he'd clapped eyes on his fraternal uncle, at the second he'd repaid the debt he owed the old man for raising him, when he saved Bill from being worked to death by the outriders. He'd made good on his mistakes, for what it was worth. Hadn't he?

Tyler pulled a sour face. There was nothing like sitting alone in a darkened room for making you doubt yourself all over again.

The blanket over the doorway eased open a crack and Bill Tyler entered, a smile on his weather-beaten old face. "Hey there, lad. You've got some colour in your cheeks now."

"Yeah. Reckon I'll be fit to ride tomorrow."

The old man looked away for a second. "You given any thought to where you'll be going?"

Tyler's voice caught in his throat. "I – I'm not sure..."

Bill sat at his side. "Son, I learnt when you were fifteen years old that the time when I could tell you what to do with yourself had passed. I did my best to give you the mind and the common sense to make your own choices and, God willing, to make them good ones."

"I know that. I owe what I am to you."

"And what is that, Gabriel? You're reckless and impulsive, bull-headed and full of yourself..." The old man laughed. "Heck, you're the very mirror of me!"

They shared a smile. "I want to thank you for coming after me, son," Bill said quietly. "There were times in that damnable place when I thought I would never see another day of freedom again." He patted Tyler's chest. "You've got a good heart, a strong will, and for that I'm as proud as I can be."

"I knew I had to get you out of there. That's all that I had on my mind."

"But what now?" Bill asked. "You did your duty to your kin, so I guess you'll be riding home to Stonetree with Tulsa and me? Lord knows, she and I both want you to, safe and outta harm's way..."

Tyler studied his uncle. The wily old coot knew just what was running through his mind, the doubts that he held. "Fivehawk says that Drache's still out there," he said after a moment. "He tells me that the man's made a pact with a devil, or some-such. I don't rightly understand it myself, but..."

189

"But what?"

"He says that he can't beat Drache alone ... but he's got all these stories about monsters with no faces falling outta the sky, and there's these men with green blood and all kinds of crazy scientification..." Tyler broke off. "It's all too strange to me."

Bill nodded slowly. "Gabe, after working in that mine I reckon I believe in monsters sure enough, but that ain't what matters. It don't matter what Fivehawk calls a demon or whatever his redskin legends say it is – what matters is that you, lad, know what the difference is between good and evil. And I taught you that as soon as you were old enough to talk."

"You did indeed," Tyler said with a smile.

"Devil or not, that rattlesnake Drache is as evil a man as has ever walked the face of the West, and you know that as well as Fivehawk does."

Tyler had a sudden flash of realization. "He hasn't come to see me because he's not sure I'll come with him..."

Bill nodded again. "That there is a choice you've got to make. Indian legends and the words of an old fool like me don't count for squat, boy. You just do what's right." His uncle got up and ruffled his hair. "And don't be staying in bed all day! Ain't got no use for..."

"...a lazy dog!" said Tyler, recalling the hundreds

190

of times his uncle had used those words to rouse him as a child.

The old man winked and left him alone with his thoughts.

When dawn rose the next day, Jonathan Fivehawk rose with it, his saddlebags packed with supplies and his horse fed and watered. He patted the animal's chestnut nose and whispered to him a few words of encouragement. He drank in a deep breath and looked up at the sky. It would be a beautiful day today. Fivehawk led his horse from the escapee camp, pausing to thank Tall Tree once again for his help, and nodding to Tulsa as she drew water from the well. When he reached the entrance to the valley, Grey Arrow and Rivercloud were blocking his way, and Looks-Far stood off to one side, a cloth sack in his hand.

"You're taking your leave of us, then?" said the Elder.

Fivehawk nodded. "I have no more call to rest on your hospitality. The stars do not wait." He jerked his chin at the lightening sky, indicating a trio of stars clustered close together. "I must seek The Faceless before they are as one."

Rivercloud impulsively stepped forwards and planted a kiss on Fivehawk's cheek. "Thank you, Wanderer, for reminding me how important my home is."

Grey Arrow smiled broadly, despite the flash of jealousy from Looks-Far. "I thank you too, Fivehawk. In turn, you showed me not to fear the unknown."

"We have gifts for you," Looks-Far said, holding up the sack, "some tools that may aid you in your fight against The Faceless."

Fivehawk opened the bag and peered inside; he drew out a handful of stone arrowheads and bullets. At first he thought they were common enough, but the glint of the sun flashed jade green off their tips. "Sky rock?" he asked.

Rivercloud nodded. "Some of the prisoners managed to take some before the earthquake destroyed the storehouse."

He bowed his head in thanks. "These will be a great help in defeating any Guardians and Drache's minions. Thank you all." Fivehawk faltered; he felt he should say something more, but no words came to mind.

"Going somewhere?" asked a voice.

Fivehawk turned to see Tyler and his uncle approaching, with the girl Tulsa leading his horse behind them. The Indian suppressed a smile and studied him levelly.

"I've learnt Drache is building a railroad out to the north. Perhaps I may be able to find my sister there."

Tyler pushed back his hat with an index finger. "You want some company?"

"What about your uncle?"

Bill smiled and gestured to Tulsa. "I reckon I can look after myself from here on in. Muriel here will make sure of that." Tulsa shot him a look but said nothing.

Fivehawk mounted his horse and Tyler followed suit. "You helped me find my kin when he was lost," the cowboy said, "I guess I owe you the same courtesy. And maybe, two motivated young men might be able to take this here fight to Mister Drache himself..." Tyler's horse ambled up alongside Fivehawk's. "Unless, of course, you don't think a paleface is of any use to you," he added.

A smile tugged at the corners of Fivehawk's mouth. "You can join me," he said, "and perhaps I can teach you to control that impulsive streak of yours!"

"It's a deal!" Tyler gave Tulsa a wink, let out a whoop and saluted the assembled crowd with his hat. "Let's ride!"

With a crack of reins, they urged their mounts into a gallop, and bolted through the mouth of the valley and into the land beyond, into the growing brightness of the new day.

Targa's escape had been a long, extended race across barren desert and arid scrubland, nights spent hidden in the lee of boulders or concealed in gullies for fear that the slaves might come after her, hunt her down; or worse, that Trebuchet's twisted self might have some how survived the earthquake that claimed the Burnt Hills. But a colder, deeper fear had gripped her as she crested a rise to discover Drache's steam engine, the monstrous Black Train, lurking silently just over the horizon, waiting on the bright steel tracks like a dozing predator, with its bullet prow pointed out into the widening vista of the desert. Leaving her spent horse behind, she'd stumbled to the carriage, half in real exhaustion and half as an act, wailing for help. Two new outriders she'd never met before brought her aboard the train, and the moment they kicked the door closed behind her, the huge machine began moving, quickly picking up speed.

It seemed as if Drache had been waiting here for her to arrive — but how could that be? How would he have known? They left her, still breathing hard, in the library carriage. She glanced around. Nothing had changed, the same endless racks of strange, arcane books, rolled texts and parchments, walls with maps of unknown lands and paintings of severe men with hawkish eyes — and there, in the corner, a brass pole with a horizontal cross-bar. Targa got up, careful to keep exaggerating her fatigue. Something was attached to the bar, a black clump of rags the size of her head...

When she was about to touch them, the rags flapped open into the shape of an enormous crow.

The bird squawked and snapped at her with its beak; Targa hissed and spat back at it, like an angry cat. She noticed a thick, heavy pendant around the crow's neck, a bulky instrument of some kind. It took a moment for her to recognize the device — it was a wireless telegraph of Drache's invention, which communicated words and pictures in some cryptic manner.

"They make the best spies," said Drache.

Targa whirled around in fright, composing herself a second later. "Oh, Robur!" she cried. "It was awful! Trebuchet ... he tried to ... wanted to ... turn me against you!" She fell into his arms, and he cradled her there.

"Indeed?" he said mildly. "Do go on." He began to guide her along the carriage, towards the opposite end.

"The jewel you asked us to find, he took it and perverted it! His only desire was power, my Master. Power to destroy you!" Targa poured her heart and soul into her performance.

Drache nodded carefully. "Trebuchet wanted to be like me, did he?"

"Oh yes, Robur. He coveted your relationship with ... our benefactor."

"And you, my dearest Targa? Did you too want to take my place?"

She shook her head violently. "Oh no..." she said, and fell silent. Drache was leading her into the carriage of the train which contained his study, where he never let any outrider enter. She froze, but he continued to walk her forward, with gentle but firm pressure. She knew at that moment that he saw through her. The crow, the damnable crow must have been his eyes and ears while he had left them alone, spying on them.

Drache planted a kiss on her cheek. "You are so poor a liar in my eyes, Targa," he said, removing his obsidian glasses. Underneath, where other men had flesh and blood sight organs, Drache's eyeballs were cast of solid brass, with delicate metallic filigree around glassy lenses.

Targa's duplicity died in her throat. She shook her head. "No…"

With a sudden, violent shove, Drache threw her into the study and she collapsed to the floor. "Your greed for my power has made you stupid and clumsy, Targa," he said, his voice rising. "Trebuchet paid for that with his life, destroying years of my work in moments! A punishment must be exacted in return!"

Targa got to her knees. "Please, my Master. I beg of you, spare me!"

"I'm not going to kill you!" he said with a sharp laugh. "What kind of man would do that to a defenceless woman?" His tones turned icy. "No, I see that all you require is a lesson in humility."

Drache gestured to an object on a table; a flawless sphere of some strange, unknown material — the

196

device he called The Instrument. "My father once made me drink an entire bottle of whiskey because he caught me stealing a single sip. I caught you sipping at my hegemony, so now you will learn the lesson I did..."

Targa had seen a million cruel and terrible things in her life, and had done most of them herself; but still, her heart froze when the sphere split open, spilling a terrifying, unearthly light around the walls. Light of a kind very similar to that she had seen in the underground chamber.

"See what I see, Targa. Witness the glory of The Faceless."

A thousand brass cables erupted from the sphere, fast as swarming wasps, and flew at her face, cutting, probing, slicing towards the soft tissues of her eyes.

SUNDOWNERS

Watch out for
the next book in the series

IRON DRAGON

The sky was a vast cowl of grey, oily wool strung out over the mountaintops, the invisible sun casting a weak light in all directions across the hardened, chilled landscape. The work camp had been in this spot for a little over nine days now, the labourers slaving under the shadow of the mountain the white men called Frost Peak, the endless grind of stone and the clanking of metal against metal echoing around them. Yu Lim peered out from under her battered straw hat and shivered. Here in this place, there was never enough warmth to go around, never enough food or water. This land, this America, was a cold, cold place, and not for the first time she longed for feel of her homeland beneath her feet instead of this iron-hard earth. Hundreds of her people were here, silently carrying out their duties, gradually assembling the lengths of steel track and wooden sleepers, building the railroad that wandered back and forth through the foothills. She moved quickly between the shacks and tents that formed the camp's nucleus, vanishing into shadows whenever one of the lumbering hulks that guarded them hove into view. Yu Lim allowed herself a small smile. From the day she joined the ship at Shanghai, she had made herself invisible to these overseers, these outriders. The teachings of her elderly *sifu*, her teacher, were second nature to her now, and she could make her footsteps quieter than a cat's, should she desire.

But she had wasted too much time; Yu Lim had allowed herself to become distracted by her concerns for her brothers and sisters, who slaved and slowly died as they forged the iron road – and for what? The railroad led nowhere, it did nothing. She shook off the thoughts, blinking them away like tears from her eyes. Her purpose here was clear, and it was time for her to fulfil it.

Tong Biao was a stocky, middle-aged man with wide eyes and an easy smile, even in a place like this, and he never failed to make Yu Lim grin whenever she stole out of the shadows. Startled, he coughed and blinked, and caught a squeal of alarm in his throat.

"Yu Lim, you are a demon child!" he hissed. "Why do you find such amusement in scaring me?"

"Ah Tong, I take a smile where I can."

"Indeed." He nodded, then looked away. "Come, then. Let's do this before I change my mind."

Tong led Yu Lim to a canvas-covered wagon stacked with long cloth sacks. The girl shuddered at the sight of them; each one contained a corpse, a worker who had fallen victim to an "accident" or other misadventure. From the back of the wagon emerged Sing Lung, a younger man closer to Yu Lim's age, but worn down by a life of hard toil.

"More victims of the sickness," Sing said carefully.

Yu Lim nodded. All through the camp, the workers whispered about a disease, unseen and deadly, that stalked them. Its prey would slowly sicken and die, as if the very *qi* – the essence of life – was siphoned from them.

"Where should I hide myself?" she asked, putting aside her concerns.

Tong Biao shifted from foot to foot and shook his head. "This is not right. You are a child. You should not be here."

"I have no choice," she said carefully, and sighed. "Ah Tong, we have had this argument a hundred times and still you wish to have it again."

"She knows what she must do," Sing Lung broke in, producing an empty sack.

"I do," Yu Lim said, and she leant close to Tong. "Trust in Heaven." She planted a kiss on his cheek and stepped into the sack. "Quickly, now. Red-hair will be here soon."

Sing Lung took a quick look around to make sure no one was watching them, then pulled the sack up around her. He paused before closing it over her head. "Do you have it?" he asked.

She nodded, showing the tip of a long object wrapped in cloth, hidden in the folds of her jacket. "It has never left my hands."

He nodded and closed the sack over her. His pleasant face now a scowl, Tong Biao took Yu Lim's legs while Sing Lung held her arms, and they gently placed her atop the pile of the dead.

"Good luck, little sister," Tong mumbled.

"The nimble foot gets in first." Yu Lim's voice was muffled, but it carried an edge to it. "Fear not for me, my friend. I have no path other than this one."

Tong opened his mouth to say something else, but Sing Lung grabbed his arm and pulled him away. "The Red-hair is here!"

They rode into the camp on five horses all black as pitch. At the fore, two outriders cast watchful stares out over the workers as they paused in their labours, and riding behind was a trio of women. Sitting high in the saddle, Red-hair's flame-coloured tresses cascaded down her back like a fiery waterfall, fanned out over the long ebony leather coat she wore. The sight of the woman always disturbed Tong Biao; a thick blindfold covered her eyes and yet she moved as if she could see more than any of them. The outriders dismounted, and then the other two females, before Red-hair stepped down. Tong studied the women. They were similar in stature, long and willowy in a way that the girls he'd chased during his youth in Canton never were. One was as pale as milk, with a face framed by yellow curls, the other tawny-skinned with dark hair. Both of them had eyes that pierced anyone who met their gaze.

Red-hair was speaking to another outrider, a bearded man who seemed only shades away from an animal up on its hind legs. "Grizzly, you have done well. Master Drache is pleased with your work here."

The outrider scratched at his face. "I work these Chinee real good, Ma'am."

"You do. We will soon be finished."

Tong Biao's heart jumped in his chest. Finished soon? Then perhaps he could still save Yu Lim from her dangerous outing...

Sing Lung's hand clamped around his arm. "Stop it, Ah Tong! I know what you are thinking! Don't let your feelings cloud your judgement!"

One of the outriders began to hitch his horse to the canvas wagon, and he gave the two men a sneering glance.

Tong rounded on the younger man and snarled, "She's just a girl! Someone filled her head with silly stories, made her come halfway around the world, and for what? Enough of our people have come here and died here, so why add another?" He spat. "When we came to this America, we called this place the Land Without Ghosts because no Chinese had been buried here, but that's not true any more! We're filling it up with our dead!" He pointed at the wagon. "She'll join them!"

Sing Lung cast a nervous glance at the outrider, then back to Tong. "Quiet, you old fool! No man can argue against the orders of Heaven! You'll draw them here and they will kill her for certain!"

The anger suddenly fled from Tong Biao. "Oh, Ancestors. What am I doing?"

"Dawne, what are they saying?" Red-hair's voice demanded. Sing and Tong froze.

The pale woman studied them. "I'm not sure. Something about death."

"Indeed?" Red-hair said nothing, but the dark-skinned woman stepped closer to examine the wagon. Red-hair nodded. "Perhaps they are mourning a friend? Duske, we wouldn't want to send anyone to their grave before their time, would we?"

The dark female nodded, and drew a thin, rapier-like blade from a scabbard under her coat. Sing caught a glimpse of a strange, jewelled clasp in the woman's hair before she stepped on to the wagon, and drove the blade hilt-deep into one of the corpses. Then the next. And the next.